THE ANCIENT EGG

XENO-SPECTRE
BOOK 2

MARY E. LOWD

For Amy and Trudy

1

Their wings fill my nightmares, and nightmares fill my sleep. I close my eyes, and I see my loved ones—my daughters, my family—frozen in place, their faces twisted, painted on metal wings. Smaller metal wings flutter around me, sharp-edged, sharp as knives, cutting at my face and hands. Under it all, under my own skin, I feel lumps moving—tiny legs crawling, eating my body from the inside out, ready to burst out from my skin, leaving me shredded.

I don't sleep well. Not anymore. Not since our visit to that hell moon.

I left one of my daughters there—an uplifted dog named Gaby, who I'd had cloned and raised from the time she was a puppy small enough to sleep cupped in my two hands. I didn't even get to bury her, just leave her body behind, discarded but not forgotten.

Gaby comes to me in my dreams too, and somehow, those dreams are worse than the nightmares, because I wake up from them shattered. My grief for her as fresh as it was a year ago, right after she died. I lose her over and over again, every time I sleep, every time my unconscious brain tricks me into forgetting that she's gone.

At the time, I'd had only one other daughter—an uplifted cat who I adopted as a teenager. She's snarky, independent, and everything a cat should be. Now I have three daughters—Cristobel, the cat; Maya, a human girl who we rescued from the ruins of a religiously extremist society on Hell Moon; and Jaimy, an adult uplifted dog who lost her human guardian at the same time as I lost Gaby. Apparently, I like to take in foundlings.

The four of us live together on a sentient spaceship called *The Kanga*.

I also have two sons—mere babes, recently hatched from the ancient eggs we found on Hell Moon, where Gaby died. My daughters are helping me care for them.

The weird thing about going to hell and back—even if you suffer an unutterable loss along the way—is that you can't quite entirely regret it... not if you come away from hell with whole new people in your life—brand new, just hatched from their eggs people, who look at you with wide, naive, sweet eyes. Never mind that those eyes are a little creepy with narrowed slits of pupils inside the rich, speckled purple of a nebula that never stops staring at you because s'rellick don't have eyelids.

You think it's hard to get a mammalian baby to go to sleep? Try it with a reptilian babe who can't close their eyes, and they just keep staring sightlessly at you after they've drifted off, so you never quite know when it happens. That restful moment of release when the baby's eyes slowly close and you know they're asleep never comes. However, you can keep staring at those beautiful eyes, wondering at how an entire nebula can fit in a child's eye while the scaly babe breathes deeply, sleeping in your arms.

I would never have traded Gaby for two reptilian s'rellick

babes. But now that T'ni and A'nu are in my life, I also wouldn't trade them.

It's a horrible contradiction. Love ends, and new love begins. And both of them leave indelible scars on your soul, defining you.

Sometimes I think about how much Gaby would have loved playing with T'ni and A'nu. But I try not to. I don't want to cry that much.

Gaby had talked about raising a cloned puppy of her own some day—uplifted cats and dogs don't live as long as humans, so she'd have partly been raising a grandchild for me and partly raising her own replacement.

As it is, I don't think I could raise a puppy again. And I wouldn't have chosen to be raising T'ni and A'nu, except their eggs were aboard my ship, entrusted to me by the s'rellick team who unearthed them and lost their lives with Gaby. Someone had to raise the reptile boys, and as I understand it, s'rellick basically abandon their eggs in a warm cave, throw some food in there every so often, and wait to see which hatchlings eventually emerge from childhood still alive to become full adults. I couldn't do that to T'ni and A'nu... not after so much was lost, so many lives paid for rescuing them from Hell Moon where they'd been aging, too cold to hatch, for nearly a century.

They were so ready to hatch, as soon as we turned up the temperature in *The Kanga's* room where we were storing them, the leathery shells of their eggs began to crack before we even finished the week-long flight back to Fathomscape Station.

We've been docked at Fathomscape ever since, living off the money *The Kanga* earned from the s'rellick—who all died—on their mission to Hell Moon.

I have nightmares about them too—I had to kill one of them with my own hand. I pulled a trigger, and the lizard died, only to rise as a ghost who must still walk the abandoned corridors of the ruined colonies, built one atop another on Hell Moon. I dream that her ghost has found a way to cross hyperspace and has come to Fathomscape to steal T'ni and A'nu away from me. She's come to haunt me and critique every choice I make as a parent.

In a way, she does haunt me. I see Ahn'ssi's judgmental gaze in the eyes of every s'rellick I pass aboard Fathomscape Station. I know they're bewildered by the way my family is raising these two s'rellick toddlers. But they don't interfere—my sons are marked as different by the iridescent marbled color of their scales. They hatched from aged, ancient eggs that had allowed them an extra century to bake and develop before hatching. They're different. Special. And the normal s'rellick who see my sons lower their gaze in an almost reverential way. It's very strange—like I'm raising tiny religious figures to a society I barely know.

I walk through the gently curving corridors of Fathomscape's middle ring with one scaly talon in each of my hands. T'ni and A'nu walk on either side of me. My adopted human daughter, Maya, prances ahead of us, skipping and hopping over seams in the metal floor in some kind of complicated game that exists only inside her own head. Above our heads, windows stretch out forward and backward, showing the stars outside and the curve of the station's innermost ring above us. The ring we're on is filled with alien lifeforms of all kinds— humans, s'rellick, avian aliens, other mammaloid aliens, and even insects. The innermost ring, however, belongs exclusively to a hive of moth-like aliens called the Ll'th'th.

Overall, Fathomscape is a human space station, designed by and for humans. However, the white dwarf Fathomscape orbits is low on planetary satellites and has only a limited asteroid belt that was mostly mined out long ago. Thus Fathomscape Station struggles from existing in a relatively poor star system. When the Ll'th'th hive offered to purchase an entire ring of the floundering space station several generations ago, it injected sorely needed resources into the system, and their continued presence has allowed Fathomscape to thrive. I learned all about it in history classes as a kid.

Cristobel asks me sometimes whether the moth-like Ll'th'th bother me, after our experience with the murderous, rampaging scarabs on Hell Moon. I guess, based on how many times she's asked, that they must bother her. And it's true that both the Ll'th'th and the scarabs are insectile races, but they couldn't seem more different to me.

The scarabs in my nightmares and back on that moon are hard as rocks, with wings of sheet metal, sharp as knives along the edges. Their faces are inscrutable smooth stretches of obsidian with eyes that burn like embers and wriggling mouth parts at the base of saw-like mandibles. Everything about them screams—*murder! danger! run! hide! or you'll die!*

The Ll'th'th are pastel, candy-colored, fuzzy, cuddly fairy elves in comparison. Their faceted eyes look like sparkly disco balls, and their proboscis tongues curl up like crazy straws. Feathered antennae rise above their heads like some kind of crown, and their colorful wings drape over their backs like capes. Their bodies are covered in fur, making them almost seem mammalian. I mean, obviously, they're not. They're insects with a hive-based social structure. I think there's a queen somewhere in that inner ring and a bunch of lounging drones. Although, non-Ll'th'th aliens like me certainly never see them, so I'm just guessing. On the middle and outer ring, we just see the worker-sisters who take jobs among the rest of us to bring money back to their hive.

Maybe part of my comfort with the moth-like Ll'th'th comes from the fact that I grew up here on Fathomscape Station, so they seem perfectly normal to me. Just part of the crowd. Cristobel, on the other hand, was raised as a companion for a human child on a long space mission on a small ship like *The*

Kanga, with just a couple humans around. She was already a teen by the time her origin-family—the ones who cloned her in the first place—dumped her on Fathomscape, and I adopted her. So, she's not as used to all the bustle and noise, all the chaos and confusion of different species living together. Me? I love it. It makes me feel safe, knowing all these other people are here and feel safe. I guess it's like I feel like the entire universe is a coal mine, but as long as I'm surrounded by enough canaries, I should be okay.

Sometimes though, for Cristy's sake, I wish we could afford to move to an actual planet. Somewhere with fields of grass and wide stretches of sky. You know, the stuff you see in movies. I think she'd like that, and it would certainly be more like what Maya grew up with on Hell Moon before the scarabs emerged and turned it into hell, killing her whole family, her whole society, and eating away the metal until only the wood and plastic bones of their buildings were left.

I shudder at the memory of being there. I do that some-times now—just shudder sometimes, out of nowhere. Neither of the lizard children holding my hands notice, or if they do, it doesn't trouble them. They're used to their adoptive-mother shuddering randomly all the time, plagued by flashbacks and irrational fears.

It's funny—my two s'rellick babes are the only part of our family that wasn't traumatized by their time on that moon, even though they were there the longest. Their eggs were laid long before Maya's parents even came to that moon, and they slept away in their eggs there through the rise and fall of two civiliza-tions, totally unscathed by the wars fought around and above them. And now they're here, pulling my hands, yanking me toward whatever shiny things catch their creepy unblinking eyes. But I keep guiding them, avoiding the food carts and trinket stalls. We have a mission today. It's not like the mission that took my family to Hell Moon. It's much smaller, safer, and more pedestrian, but after the last few days of watching these lizard toddlers, who just learned to walk with their scaly legs, bounce off the walls inside *The Kanga*, it's a mission that feels infinitely important.

I'm taking them to a toddler playgroup.

Maya hasn't been to this playgroup before; I haven't been to it since Gaby was little, right around the time I first adopted Cristobel. We stopped going shortly after that, since Gaby didn't need it as much once she had a feline sister to play with at home in our rented quarters. I know it's going to bring up weird echoes for me coming back to it again. Without Gaby.

But Maya, with the boldness of a nine-year-old, leads the way. She looked at the station map on *The Kanga's* computers before we left—she's really taken to the computer systems here —and leads us as confidently as if she had been coming to this group through her whole childhood.

The entrance to the toddler play area is a small room behind the general playground—a cordoned off section of the station's ring with brightly colored climbing structures and translucent domes of low gravity where children can float and flip and fly. There's even a carousel with little one-person rocket ships for kids to ride as they move up and down and all around in circle after circle. For the right fee. All of the structures cost credits. I've heard there are space stations where the play areas are free. That's not Fathomscape. Everything here costs money.

I pay the fee for all of us to enter the playground—me, Maya, and the two s'rellick babes—and then I pay a fee again when we get to the special room for toddlers.

This room has lots of building blocks and toys scattered over its brightly colored carpets, but no real climbing structures or any of the low gravity domes. Everything is small and simple in here, built on a scale designed to interest children who've barely realized there's a world beyond the reach of their small arms.

I find a nice spot on a particularly plush patch of carpet and sit down crosslegged. T'ni climbs into my lap, which doesn't surprise me. He hatched from the smaller of the ancient eggs we saved from Hell Moon. I was told by the s'rellick scientists who helped rescue his egg that he would be a runt. They'd have probably left his egg behind, only being interested in the bigger, healthier egg A'nu eventually hatched from.

A'nu charges off into the crowd of toddlers of all species, and Maya follows close behind him, ready to catch the toddling lizard if he falls. The two of them—nine-year-old human and nine-month-old s'rellick—join a group of mostly mammalian toddlers building a tower from bright blue foam blocks. I notice one of the toddlers, though, instead of being covered in fur is covered in feathers. An avian child. I hope A'nu and the avian hit it off. I've already seen that my adopted s'rellick children have trouble connecting with similarly aged mammals. Perhaps an avian child will click better with them.

In spite of Fathomscape Station being largely populated by the insectile Ll'th'th and also a large number of s'rellick, most of the toddlers here with their parents are mammals.

I know that s'rellick keep their children in hatching caves, so it's no surprise that T'ni and A'nu are the only lizards here. The Ll'th'th must keep their children on the inner ring, so I've never seen one. At least... I don't think I have.

I find myself peering at a child who's just approached A'nu—it's pale and tube-like with little stubby arms all along its sides. Kind of like a caterpillar, I guess. Maybe it's a baby Ll'th'th? But just looking at it makes me shudder. It reminds me of the maggots painted on the wings of the scarabs who murdered my daughter; the maggots drawn in their frescoes and murals; and the maggots I saw in my vision of their home world when one of their ghosts walked right through me. The pale-skinned maggots are the other half of the scarabs' lifecycle. I never saw one in person, but the scarabs who haunted and hunted us on Hell Moon wouldn't exist without them.

I shiver at the memories and wrap my arms tight around T'ni, who's still in my lap. I start looking around the room, my eyes darting from one parent to the next, irrationally searching for one of the scarabs who haunt my dreams. I start to shift my weight, getting ready to stand up, grab my other two children and run if we need to...

But then I see a Ll'th'th with her pastel pink-and-green wings, like spring vines and cotton candy, reach toward the tubular child, scooping it up with four stick-like arms and dragging it away from the rowdiness of the group around the tower of blue building blocks.

A couple of uplifted puppies have gotten into a wrestling match and are knocking children and foam blocks everywhere. Gaby would have been right in the middle of that tumble when she was a puppy. A'nu on the other hand has stepped back, reluctant to engage in something so physical, much like the tubular child who's now cowering in the cradling, angular arms of its Ll'th'th parent. The Ll'th'th is even soothing the tubular child with her long proboscis, which has uncurled and is playing over the child's odd face made from wriggling mouth parts and wide eyes like a human might soothe their child by stroking a hand over its hair.

The tubular child is a caterpillar. A Ll'th'th caterpillar. Nothing more. *Nothing less*, I suppose, as I realize just how rare and fascinating it is to see one. It shouldn't scare me. It's not the harbinger of scarabs come to rip my family to pieces.

Just a child, who happens to share a vaguely similar biology. I might as well be afraid of all bipedal mammals because a human once hurt me as be afraid of that little caterpillar child.

And yet. It creeps me out, summoning memories I don't want to remember.

I wonder why they're here —the caterpillar and its moth-like parent. I wonder why I've never seen a Ll'th'th caterpillar before. If it's not weird for them to be here, then why don't I see Ll'th'th leading their little tubular caterpillars around the middle ring of Fathomscape Station all the time?

And that's when the lights go out.

All of the lights.

Leaving a roomful of toddlers and their parents in utter darkness.

I look up at the windowed ceiling and see that even the inner ring where the Ll'th'th colony lives has gone dark. I can't see light anywhere, except for the distant pinpricks of stars, too far away to illuminate anything here.

One of the babies screams; it sounds like the avian child from the squawking quality of its voice. After the scream breaks the ice, a bunch of the uplifted puppies start yipping and howling. Adults are trying to shush the children, feeling their way through the dark, unsure as to whether we should wait for our eyes to adjust—wondering if they even will or if the darkness is too complete—before trying to protectively gather up our children.

The children are startled by the darkness. The adults—at least, if I'm anything to go by—are emotionally frozen, waiting to see if the lights will come back on; waiting to see if emergency lights will start flashing; waiting to hear if sirens are going to start blaring.

Blackouts in space are no joke. Life in space is entirely dependent on your spaceship or space station's life support. Without it, you freeze, overheat, or asphyxiate, depending on what your most immediate problem is. That's it. That's the deal. It's death in every direction.

That's why a space station like Fathomscape has layer after layer of backup systems, and the fact that somehow, enough of them have been knocked out at once for the toddler room in the playground area to be experiencing a blackout this complete is the kind of shocking that makes your insides turn cold and wibbly.

It's the kind of situation that makes you wonder: do I have hours left to live? Or only minutes?

...or will this be my final thought?

2

I wrap my arms tighter around T'ni, who's gone so still in my lap that he could be a statue of a child or a very realistic doll. I don't know if he's responding to my own stillness, mirroring me, or if it's an innate, reptilian reaction to the dark. In my experience so far, these reptilian children are much better at holding still than Gaby, an uplifted puppy, ever was. But when they move, they move fast.

Suddenly, something slams into my side, and reaching through the dark to feel, I find it's A'nu. He clings to my arm with small, scaly hands. A few moments later, I feel human hands on my shoulder—it's Maya. She's found her way to us, and all my children are here with me in the dark. I can feel them. I can hold on to them. That won't actually make a difference if the whole space station is dead in space, but it feels, viscerally, like now I can use my body to keep them safe. As if my human meat and bones could shield them from asphyxiation or heat death as the rest of the bodies on this station use up the air and convert it to excess heat that the life support systems are no longer shedding safely into space.

The heat will have nowhere to go. I feel a prickle of fear or sweat at the back of my neck and imagine I'm already feeling the heat levels beginning to rise.

Or maybe it's just Maya breathing down my neck, squishing herself up against my backpack, probably smashing all the sandwiches I packed inside.

"What's happening?" she asks. "Why'd it go dark?" Her voice sounds louder in the dark than it probably should. Most of the children here aren't old enough to ask coherent questions like that, being just toddlers. And all the adults are keeping to quiet, cooing, comforting sounds, hoping if they stay quiet, an announcement will come over the station-wide speakers, explaining what's going on and how it'll all be back to normal soon.

"I don't know, but I'm sure it'll be okay," I say to Maya, reassuring myself as much as the kids. Trying not to feel like I'm lying. Trying not to let the dark and the specter of rising heat send me back in my mind to Hell Moon where we ran from terrifying, giant scarabs in dark tunnels deep underground and then the double sun threatened to bake us to death before we could escape on *The Kanga*.

Dark and heat. I have trauma around those things. And a gnawing part in the back of my mind is wondering: *could it be scarabs?* Eating away at the metal of the space station? Destroying essential systems and munching on wiring? Could we have brought one back with us, in spite of *The Kanga* sterilizing herself by blasting her insides with the vacuum of space?

It can't be that. It couldn't be. It's been nearly a year. If we'd brought a scarab back with us, surely, it would have caused problems before now.

I wish I were back on *The Kanga* right now. Her metal halls and rooms are the one place in the universe where I truly feel safe anymore—because I know, she can engage her engines and blast us away from any danger, and I trust her to do that. I trust her as much as any of my children. She's part of our family. But right now, she's a twenty minute walk through the halls, elevators, and probably panicking crowds of Fathomscape Station away. And that's assuming we can see well enough to keep from getting lost.

There is one thing that was better back on Hell Moon—I was loaded up with gear. Guns, blasters, flamethrower, knives, flashlight—the whole soldier-for-hire kit. As much gear as I could carry on my body. But here? Where I'm theoretically safe and just raising a bunch of weird, foundling kids who've become part of my family?

All I've got is my wrist computer, a backpack full of snacks and toddler toys, and three kids clinging to my arms and back. No weapons. All the rest of my gear is packed away in a safe on *The Kanga*, where foolish children won't accidentally mess with it.

As my eyes adjust to the blackness, I notice a subtle glow— the s'rellick child squeezed tightly in my arms, T'ni has glowing scales. How had I never noticed that before? I guess it's never been dark enough. I look to the side, and sure enough, A'nu's scales glow dully too. I can see their shapes as ghostly outlines. It makes me shiver, reminding me of what happened to the lead researcher on the mission where we rescued their ancient eggs.

S'rellick ghosts had haunted the caverns under the surface of that moon for centuries before we got there. And Ahn'ssi must be haunting those halls with her ghostly blue energy still.

I hate seeing my sons like this. It makes them look dead and gone to me. I don't want that. I want the lights to come back on even more now, not just because I'm worried about dying in space, but because I want to see my sons in all their firm solidity. I want to see that they're real and alive and can't walk right through me. I want their ghostly, pearlescent glowing to go away.

I look away from my s'rellick sons and peer into the darkness of the rest of the room—I see more bioluminescence out there. Big swooping shapes that glow a dull green with little rosettes of pink, entirely unlike the nebular pearlescence of my sons' scales, full of too many shimmering shades to pin their color down.

I can't figure out what the swooping greens and pink rosettes are coming from, but then, thankfully, little lights start to twinkle on around the room, breaking up the darkness. Various parents have grown impatient, waiting for the power to come back, and have turned on the flashlight apps in their wrist computers. It's still dark, but compared to the utter blackness before, this is nothing.

Now I can see that the swooping green shapes are the outline of the Ll'th'th's wings; the pink rosettes are decorative patterns on her dusky cloak of wings. I hadn't realized Ll'th'th glowed in the dark. I guess I've never been in a situation to discover it before. I wish I weren't in a situation to know about it now.

With small beams of light breaking up the darkness, some of the toddlers grow brave and go back to playing again. Some of their plastic toys add to the light, flashing and singing as plastic toddler toys are known to do. The kind of sudden, epilepsy-causing flashes and ear-splitting jingles that make adults everywhere hate that kind of toy. Right now, it's kind of comforting. The noise and chaos staves off the deadly emptiness of outer space through the windows above.

Still clinging to my back, Maya whispers in my ear, "I have something to tell you."

My heart nearly stops. What could she have to tell me? Does she know something about the blackout? She's really good at surfing the Fathomscape Station computer forums. Maybe she knows something I don't yet... "What is it?" I ask, speaking around the lump in my throat.

"I've been reading a lot of things on the forums, and I've

been thinking about it a lot... and... this is all kind of weird for me, but..."

I have genuinely no idea where Maya is heading with this, and I wish she would hurry up. Have there been whispers on the forums about potential blackouts? Have there been rumors about Fathomscape Station's power being unreliable? Children have such a way of meandering through things, using all kinds of extra filler words and hemming and hawing, especially at the worst of times.

But I know from experience that urging her to get to the point would only throw her off track, make her start over, and drag all of this out even longer. I have to wait.

"...see, it's confusing because I know that no one on Pentathia believed in this kind of thing—" Pentathia is Maya's name for Hell Moon. I still think of it as Hell Moon though, because that's what it was to me. Pentathia was nothing more than a dead husk by the time I saw it. "—Aunty Moira would have said a devil had possessed me if I told her this, but I know she was wrong about Cristobel and Jaimy—" From what I'd learned, the colony on Pentathia had been xenophobic, deeply religious, and thought that uplifting cats and dogs was the work of the devil. They'd thought a lot of things were immoral and signs of the devil. So many that I have no clue where Maya is wending her way toward with this one-sided conversation. And I'm starting to wonder if it's even a conversation that needs to be happening right now with the lights out and imminent doom hanging over a room filled with restless toddlers and their frightened parents.

Fortunately, T'ni and A'nu are still clinging to me like little statues, perfectly still, and slightly, eerily glowing.

"I'm sorry, honey," I cut Maya off, "but I can't think very clearly right now. Could you get to the point? Is it related to the blackout?"

"The blackout?" Maya asks in confusion. I've really done it.

I've thrown her off track, and now we'll have to wind through all her concerns about what her dead Aunty Moira would think of whatever it was she wasn't saying all over again.

I only met Aunty Moira briefly before she died and became a ghost. She spent pretty much the entire time screaming. I don't feel like her opinions on much of anything really matter anymore at this point, but she was a significant part of Maya's family up until nine months ago. A kid doesn't just get over that. I'm kind of amazed Maya's been doing as well as she has, actually, given that her entire world came to an end—overnight for her, and more than a century ago to those of us who didn't spend the last hundred years sleeping in a cryotube. A lot of her resilience seems to do with the bond she's formed with Cristobel.

"I think I'm a boy," Maya says, surprising me with the simple, directness of her—his?—words.

"Is that all?" I ask, relief bubbling up inside me. Relief tinged with annoyance. How can a kid think that a time like this is a good one for... well... anything. I guess, if it's a bad time for everything, it might as well get whiled away with a conversation topic like this one.

"What makes you think you're a boy?" I ask, trying to get more information, trying to focus on this conversation instead of trying to count in my head how long the lights have been out for and start calculating how soon we should start worrying about air filters.

Should I try to walk us home to *The Kanga's* berth through the darkness? Will the doors to a room like this one be locked down in response to the blackout? Are we locked in? I need to not panic. I can't afford to panic while watching two toddlers and a nine-year-old going through an identity crisis.

In response to my question, I feel Maya, who's still clinging to my back, kind of shrug. At least, I think it's a shrug. It's hard to interpret when she—he?—is behind me, and I can't hardly see anything except a bunch of conflicting shadows and distracting points of light anyway.

"I dunno," Maya says. "I just think I might be a boy."

That's not a lot to work with, and I have no experience dealing with a trans kid. Personally, gender's never been terribly important to me, but I know it matters a lot to some people. Maybe Maya's one of those people.

On the other hand, maybe Maya's just trying to create a new identity to escape all of the pain that she—he?—has gone through in the last year. Turn herself into someone new— someone who didn't lose her parents, aunt, friends, and entire world in a brutal tragedy, followed by being frozen in a cryopod for a hundred years.

Anyone would want to escape from that identity.

That said, if gender doesn't really matter to me, then it shouldn't really matter to me whether Maya is a cis girl or a trans boy. Either way, she's Maya. Well... I mean... You know what I mean. The kid is the same person, the same kid I've been coming to love over the last nine months, regardless of what pronouns or name the kid uses.

"Do you want me to use masculine pronouns for you?" I ask.

"Uh... okay."

"Would you..." This will be harder for me. Switching pronouns is a bit of a mental trick, but when you live around a bunch of alien species who have all kinds of different life cycles and genders, sometimes switching back and forth between genders as they age, you get used to it. But changing Maya's name? I'm pretty used to thinking of Maya as Maya. But hey, with kids, you do what needs to be done. So, I grit my teeth and finish the sentence properly: "...would you like me to call you by a more masculine name? If so, would you like help picking one? Maybe..." There's nothing that says I can't try to make this as easy on myself as possible. "...maybe something kind of similar to Maya? Like, I don't know, Max?"

At least then, when I start to say "Maya," I can drag out that opening "M" until I remember to switch over and say "Max" instead. Fortunately, Maya—well, Max, I guess—goes for it.

"Yeah! Max is a cool name!"

I thought Ma— Max would like that. There's a cat named Max in one of he— his favorite cartoon sims. "You hear that, little ones?" I say to the lizard babes clinging to me. "We're gonna call your big human sibling Max now, okay? He's a boy like you." The lizard babes don't respond. They don't talk yet, not even meaningless babbling really. Just silence. I still figure it's good for us to talk to them.

I guess, one good takeaway from this conversation is that Ma— Max is so unfazed by the blackout that sh— he doesn't seem to be scared by it at all. That means he trusted me when I said it was fine. That's good. I hope I wasn't lying.

Also, damn, but it's messing with my head having to change names and pronouns every time I think about my adopted nine-year-old. But it has distracted me, at least briefly, from much more important questions.

Questions like, why hasn't some sort of backup power brought the lights back on by now?

Stations like this always have backup systems. You can't have biological lifeforms living in the harsh emptiness of space without multiple redundant backup systems for keeping them alive. It's just not smart. And whatever else, this space station has been here, spinning and filled with people, for my whole life as well as generations and generations back before me. So, it's not like it's some untested new structure.

Maybe that's the problem. Maybe a station like this has a lifespan and I've had the misfortune of being born onto it just in time for it to fizzle out like a dying sun right while I'm trying to take my second round of adopted kids to a fun toddler playdate.

T'ni shifts on my lap, his long tail uncoiling in a way that signifies restlessness. Even lizards, preternaturally designed to hold still, get restless in the dark when they're energetic toddlers. Beside me, A'nu's little scaly hands slip off my arm, and I turn to see just where he thinks he's going in all this darkness.

A'nu has reached out and joined hands with that creepy caterpillar child. The caterpillar child has a lot of hands along its long, sinuous sides, but A'nu has clasped on to two of them. The Ll'th'th parent has moved closer to us too, standing behind her caterpillar like a good, attentive parent. I can't make out any details of her expression—not that I know how to read expressions on a Ll'th'th's face with its curled proboscis tongue and disco ball eyes. The eyes do sparkle in the dim light of the room.

"Hi," I say to her. "Our kids seem to like each other." It's such a strangely mundane, normal thing to say in this heightened situation. But I'm not sure what else to do. It's not like wailing in terror about the idea that we all might die in a matter of hours would help anything.

And of course, beneath it all, buried as deep as I can keep it, lurks the most horrible thought: could this be my fault? Could a baby scarab—one of those horrible, murderous, metal-eating creatures—have managed to survive *The Kanga* having exposed her innards to the vacuum of space?

Could one of the scarabs have hitch-hiked here with us, spent nine months nibbling on the edges of Fathomscape Station without anyone noticing, and finally have worked its way up to eating the whole central power grid, all of a sudden, with no previous warning, today?

If so, we have more problems than just a space station dying around us. We have monsters.

But that thought doesn't make any sense.

It doesn't.

It can't.

I saw the baby scarabs' shells after *The Kanga* returned from exposing them to vacuum. They were dead. I stepped on one of them and felt it crush under my foot.

"Yes," the Ll'th'th sings in Solanese, the same language as I've been speaking and also the standard on Fathomscape Station. Though, I have heard Ll'th'th speak to each other in a different language often enough to know that Solanese isn't their native tongue. Not that they have tongues, per se. Unless, I guess, those curled tube-like proboscises are technically tongues, which they might be. "My Kalithee has not shared such a shining with another pre-chrysalis one before." The Ll'th'th's voice has a musical lilt, like a flute trying to mimic human speech. It's kind of pretty.

"Kalithee?" I ask. "Is that your little one's name?"

"Yes, it's what I've been calling the child I raise."

I watch A'nu try to play a clapping game with Kalithee. It's a game Cristobel taught him, and it usually only involves four hands—two per player. With Kalithee's whole row of extra hands—or tentacles, I guess, it's hard to tell in this light—the game plays very differently, and A'nu keeps chuckling with his adorable little laugh that sounds a bit like hiccuping. It's nice to see him so happy, even if it is because he's playing with a child that still creeps me out. I'll get over it. I can do that for A'nu. Also, myself. It's not like I want to carry around trauma from Hell Moon forever.

"Maybe we should set up a playdate for our little ones sometime," I suggest to the Ll'th'th parent. She agrees and tells me her name is Kth. Then I introduce myself and my three adopted children. It's my first time introducing Maya—the kid who used to be Maya—as Max, and that feels kind of weird in my mouth, but Ma— Max does a little happy hop-skip when I use the new name, so it's worth it.

When all this settles down, I need to look into puberty blockers for Max. I honestly don't know if this is just a phase while sh- he processes the pain of all he's lost and reinvents himself or if it's truly who he's going to be for the rest of his life. But either way, puberty blockers are pretty standard for human kids these days. Who wants to deal with puberty before you're ready, right? I should probably have been looking into them already, but I'm still kind of getting used to being a parent to a human child. Uplifted cats and dogs go through fewer physical changes at puberty, so it doesn't matter as much with them. Just another on the long list of things I need to learn about now that I'm parenting a human and two s'rellick.

Kth sits down on the floor beside me, crossing her three pairs of spindly limbs, and both of my s'rellick sons play with her caterpillar child. Maya joins them. Max. I mean Max joins them. My third boy.

Finally, I get up my courage to check a few station message boards on my wrist computer. There's a lot of speculation. Wild, useless speculation. And a lot of fear—which is why I didn't check earlier; I don't need any help spiraling over this blackout situation. Personal direct messages aren't down-loading right now—the digital traffic jam of everyone panicking has clogged up the station computer systems. So, no word from Cristobel or Jaimy, but I'm sure they're fine. They're both adults, and *The Kanga* has her own power system.

I am glad that my littler kids—my sons—seem to be seeing this as a fun adventure. That's easier than dealing with scared kids on top of my own fear.

Even so, with no real clues about what's actually going on, it's time to get out of here. I gave the station a chance to get the lights back on without panicking about it. At this point, though, it's rational and not panic to insist on getting out of here. Now, it's time to get to *The Kanga* so, if push comes to shove, my whole family can make a quick exit.

We are not going down with whatever is happening here.

"Okay, kids," I say, raising my voice enough for them to hear me over the chaos of children playing in the dark. "We need to pack up and get home. Time to say goodbye to your new friend."

"Where is home?" Kth asks. The minimal light glitters off the facets of her large, silvery eyes.

"We live on a spaceship berthed in the docking section," I say, standing up and straightening the backpack on my shoulders.

"Lucky," Kth says. "Free to fly on the winds of luck."

"Something like that," I agree. "I guess you and Kalithee are part of the hive on the inner ring? I hope everything's okay there." As far as I know, all the Ll'th'th on this station are part of one giant hive.

"Hmm, yes," Kth says, humming the words. "The mother-queen sings in my mind even now. Her lullaby is scared, angry."

"You can hear her in your mind?" I'm intrigued, though this probably isn't the time to be asking anthropological questions. Maybe when we set up that hypothetical playdate—assuming the station doesn't fizzle and die first—I can learn more about the Ll'th'th from Kth. There's clearly a lot I don't know. It's amazing how you can live right next to another species for your entire life and only learn the surface things about them and their culture.

"Oh, yes," Kth says. Practically sings in her musical voice. "Mother-queen's lullaby laces through every aspect of daily life. She fills all our minds. Is how I know—she feels great responsibility for what is happening."

That stops me cold. The queen feels responsible? What does that even mean? Is it one of those feelings of vague guilt that plagues us all when something goes wrong, like if you hadn't made the mistake of thinking you were having a good day, then the universe wouldn't feel the need to smack you down? Or is there actually something the Ll'th'th queen has done to cause this extended blackout?

I've lived through blackouts on Fathomscape before. That's part of why I haven't completely lost it. Most of the other parents in this room are probably old enough to remember the blackouts that happened when I was a preschool kid and then again in high school. The first time, it was only the middle ring —where we are now—that lost power, and so we could see the comforting, steady lights of the innermost ring. I remember feeling like it was all a big adventure. That's about all I remember.

The blackout when I was in high school only affected the innermost ring, so it didn't really affect me. I just watched the ring go dark and speculated with all the other kids in my class about how long it would take for the lights to come back on.

It didn't take this long. And it wasn't both rings at once. I can't see the outermost ring—which is mostly cargo and storage and equipment—from here. It's beneath our feet. But I'd bet anything that those lights are out too.

The air in this toddler play room is already getting quite warm and stuffy. It's a small room. Hopefully, once I get my little crew out of it, the air will be a bit fresher.

Still, I'm not sure I want to lose the access I've just gained to having a clue about what's going on here. If the Ll'th'th are all telepathically connected to their queen—or empathically? I'm not sure—and she might be responsible for what's happening, then maybe I want to keep around the Ll'th'th parent who's actually interested in talking to me.

At the very least, I might hear good news faster that way. The Ll'th'th queen probably has better lines of communication open than a mere human peasant like me. She must.

"Kth," I say, "would you and Katha—" I stumble over the

caterpillar's name, partly because I can't remember it, but also because I'm looking at the child, and it still creeps me the hell out with all its pallid little tentacle arms.

"Kalithee," Kth provides helpfully.

"Right, Kalithee. Would you and Kalithee like to come back with my family for that playdate now? My spaceship has its own power, so we could wait out this blackout in comfort there." Part of me doesn't want to invite these strangers into my life and home at a critical moment like this. Could we get stuck with them? What if the station really does die, and we have to flee it—will we bring Kth and Kalithee with us? I shudder at the idea. But on the other hand, I feel like a terrible person for shuddering. Because if the station really does die, we probably ought to be inviting as many other people onboard *The Kanga* as she can reasonably fit. We'd be saving lives.

I am hating today with a passion.

How do you worry about remembering your kid's new name and manage the complexity of navigating a potential new friendship all while also worrying that everyone around you might be about to die?

At least when I was on Hell Moon, I might have been facing one life-or-death situation after another, but I wasn't also taking care of two toddlers.

But I guess I was caring for Maya. Max, dammit.

Today is the worst.

"My little pre-chrysalis one and I would love the sharing of time spent," Kth sings happily as her feathery antennae wave above her head. "We will accept your offer of kindness and hospitality."

"Great," I say, while experiencing very mixed feelings. This may have been my idea, but sometimes I have stupid ideas.

3

Once again, I stand with a lizard boy on either side of me, holding each of my hands. This time, A'nu's other hand is holding onto one of Kalithee's caterpillar hands. The two of them have become inseparable. Max prances ahead of us toward the door in the dark, just the same as before but with a different name and pronouns. Before he gets there, another parent stands up and blocks his way.

The other parent is another human, like me and Max. I come up to him and ask, "Is there a problem?"

It's hard to make out the man's face in the darkness, but I think he looks upset. That's not surprising right now. All of this is very upsetting.

He leans close to me, drops his voice to a whisper, and says, "The door's locked. Stuck. I've been trying to keep it quiet, so no one panics. But I can't get it open."

I knew this was a possibility, so I try not to feel like the station walls are closing in on me. I can see the vastness of space above me, filled with pinpoint stars, but suddenly, this room feels very, very small, and I feel like the air is getting all used up by all the other parents and their toddlers.

I need to get my family back to *The Kanga* where we have our own air scrubbers and heat recyclers, powerful enough to keep our own small group alive. Because if this blackout lasts too long, Fathomscape Station is going to turn into a hot, stuffy, ring-shaped box of carbon dioxide and dead people.

"I'd like to try it myself," I say to the man, but he steps firmly in front of me, making it clear he intends to block my way. I lower my voice and say, "I'll be subtle, okay? No one will notice if I fail, and I might succeed. I have some experience hacking door security systems."

The man grunts in an unhappy way, but he steps aside. He wants out of this room as much as I do.

A large part of me wishes I'd just grabbed his arm and twisted it behind him until he begged for mercy and let me pass without any sweet words of submission said. I could have done it. He doesn't look like he has any martial arts training, and I do. Gaby and I took classes together when she was a teen. The thought of her and those classes—us standing side by side, practicing poses—stabs me in the heart, like memories of her stab me in the heart every day. But now isn't the time to let myself get pulled down into a bog of memories.

Just like it isn't the time to start brawling with the other parents. That can come later, if this situation gets more clearly dire. Right now, we're in a liminal space where everything might still turn out okay. There might be a perfectly reasonable explanation for the blackout that we'll all hear about when it gets fixed. Any minute.

Any minute now.

While waiting for that minute, though, it's best to use my time productively. I hold my hands—still holding toddler lizard talons—out toward Max, and my older son takes the hands of my younger ones, freeing me up to examine the door.

I stand in front of the door's control panel, blocking the view of it from everyone else in the room with the placement of my body. Then I flip on the small light in my wrist computer, adjust it to a diffuse setting so it provides a glow that will help me work without shining right in my eyes and blinding me or casting stark, unhelpful shadows. It just provides a nice, steady, diffuse glow around my hands while I pry off the front cover of the door's control panel. Beneath it is a tangled nest of wires, a green motherboard, and a bunch of computer chips.

I sigh deeply. It's been years since I've hacked something like this, and a big part of me just wants to kick it as hard as I can and see if that helps. But that wouldn't be subtle, like I promised, and would probably add up to a big problem with the parent who's been guarding the door. While the darkness and fear seem to make me want to commit violence, I instead settle down into examining the different wires, trying to see which ones serve which functions and what I can possibly do to override the lockdown. Staring at the wires—trying to make out their different colored sheaths in this dim light—immediately starts to give me a headache. The sound of toddlers of all species experiencing all range of emotions behind me isn't helping either.

I keep picturing them all suffocating to death in this small room, and right now, I can't think of much worse than suffocating to death while also watching a roomful of toddlers gasping for their last breaths. Somehow, the pressure this image puts on me to get the door open isn't helping. Funny that. Sometimes pressure goads you into greater achievements than would be impossible without it... and sometimes? It just frazzles you until you fall apart.

Then, thank the heavens, the big sliding door starts to jerkily crack open, saving me from this mind-bending work. With a sigh of relief—now seems to be a time for a lot of sighing, possibly because the oxygen is getting low in here—I peer through the crack and see Gaby's wide, canine face staring back at me. My heart jumps at the sight of her. But then the vision resolves, and I see what I'm really looking at—it's Jaimy. In the dim, diffuse light from my wrist computer, she looks almost exactly like Gaby. Same height, same build, same dark fur, same wide muzzle, and same semi-flopped ears. This happens to me every week or so. I see Jaimy at an unexpected moment, and for a heartbreaking gasp's worth of time, I think I'm seeing Gaby, inexplicably returned to me. It's never more than a flash, but it always leaves me shaken. I know Gaby's never coming back. At least, most of me does. Apparently, there's a small piece, deep inside that simply doesn't understand what death means and can't accept that I left her body behind on Hell Moon, after it was thoroughly vacated and nothing more than a discarded, dog-shaped shell.

"Janice," Jaimy says to me through the crack in the door. Her paws are straining against the door and its frame, trying to shove the heavy metal door further to the side. "We came to get you. Cristobel hacked the door's lock, but it still has no power. She's trying to hook up an external battery pack, 'cause this thing is really heavy."

I haven't been paying close attention to time—doing so would only scare me—but this means the blackout's been going on for easily half an hour. Long enough for Jaimy and Cristobel to decide the rest of us needed rescuing, pack up themselves and whatever supplies they chose, hike across the station to here, and do a better job hacking the door than I'd been doing. That's not a good sign. But panicking still won't help.

"We need to get everyone out of here," I say, keeping my voice low.

The man who had been blocking the door comes over to peer past my shoulder through the crack at Jaimy, so I have no privacy in talking to her. It won't take long before other parents notice our commotion over here and the crack in the door too.

I feel a flash of pride that it's my kids who've come to rescue us all. I'm sure the other parents in this room have people worrying over them, looking for them, and probably coming to rescue them. But my Jaimy and Cristobel were the fastest, most competent of the lot. I have a good family. We're better equipped than most for handling terrifying disasters.

"What's it like out there?" I ask.

Jaimy's still straining against the door, but she relaxes her hold on it and scrunches her brow in response to my question. "Not too bad," she says. "Yet."

The door slides open, easily, without Jaimy's help, meaning Cristobel's portable battery pack must have taken over. Cristobel herself steps past the big canine. She's half Jaimy's height, even counting her tall, pointed ears. She's full-grown, but she's still about the same size as Max. "Hey, Ma," Cristobel says to me. "We're here to rescue you."

"I figured," I say, turning back toward Max and the s'rellick babes. They're all still holding hands in a row—T'ni, Max, A'nu, Kalithee, and Kth, in that order. It looks like some kind of ring-around-the-rosie game. I hope things today don't get as dark as the origins of that cute little song. "Come on," I say, gesturing for Max to bring the others forward. Then I raise my voice so the entire room can hear me: "Play time's over. We've got the door open, but it required using an external battery pack. So, you probably want to get out of here, in case the door snaps back shut when we unplug it."

Personally, I doubt that will happen. But this small room is not a good place for all these parents and small children. I'm not sure where the right place for them is... but trapped in here can't be the best option.

I get my family—plus the extra Ll'th'th parent and child we've seemingly adopted—gathered up on the outside of the door, and then I wait with Jaimy and Cristobel while everyone else files out. Jaimy hands me a pulse rifle that I sling over my shoulder, where it nestles next to my backpack of snacks and toys. Also a sheathed knife that I strap to my leg. I feel weird wielding weapons like these while also being in charge of two toddlers. I've never mixed these parts of my life—parent and lethally trained mercenary—quite so thoroughly before. But I also feel better facing a potentially lethal situation—like a blackout in space—with a couple lethal weapons by my side. And of course, Cristobel and Jaimy are even more thoroughly armed than I am.

Sometimes when people know they're about to die, they become even more dangerous than the situation that's going to kill them. I need to be able to protect my family if it comes to that. If it comes to my family or someone else, I want to be the person choosing who gets to live, and I know who I'll be choosing.

God, my body is drenched with adrenaline, isn't it? I'm all hyped up and prepared for life-or-death choices just because it's been dark for half an hour. It makes me feel like I'm the child, and my kids, who have been having a great time in all the darkness, are the actual mature ones.

After the last of the other families in the toddler playroom filter out, moving toward the larger playground, I get down on my knees beside the door and help Cristobel unhook all the wires between our briefcase-battery and the door's control panel. Like I expected, the door just sits there, continuing to gape at us like a missing tooth. I shudder.

Cristobel shoves the briefcase-battery into a backpack of her own. From the glimpse I get, it's filled with an entirely different kind of supplies than my own backpack. Rations, water packets, and weapons. Survival tools.

"Let's get back to *The Kanga*," I say. I want my whole family together. And *The Kanga* is one of us. The only one of us with her own life support system built into her body, prepared to keep all the rest of us alive.

Against squirming and complaints, I remove A'nu from

Kalithee's grasping hands and settle him on my hip. Jaimy lets T'ni crawl onto her back. Kalithee keeps standing at my feet, staring up at me with wide, pale eyes in what passes for a face at the end of her—her? I dunno—tubular body; the rows of little tentacle hands along either side of her clasp and unclasp, reaching toward the lizard child in my arms.

"We'll move faster with the little ones being carried," I say, looking pointedly at Kth. Finally the giant moth takes my hint and bundles her caterpillar up into her long, angular middle arms.

Cristobel takes Max's hand with her paw, and we're all set. Ready to go. Ready to forge our way through a darkened space station and whatever horrors it might hold.

We work our way out through the playground. There are reunions happening all around us—people finding the people they'd been separated from. Also, people wandering through the semi-darkness, calling out names, sounding half-ready to despair. I feel lucky that I have all my people with me, all of us together.

We exit the playground and enter the main thrust of the market section of the middle ring. It's better lit out here, but still dark. Hazard lights illuminate the space at regular intervals. Food stalls and other shops line either side of a wide walkway. I've walked past them a million times in my life, but they look different in the darkness and semi-illumination of the red-orange hazard lights. My home town has transformed into a completely different place.

Some of the stalls are shut down, closed up, and abandoned. Others are guarded by frantic shop owners. One mammalian alien—furry and vaguely wolf-like—argues with a group of potential customers. His stand sells frozen treats—sweet ices and chilled pastries filled with cream—but he won't sell any to the overheated patrons, even though the desserts must already be starting to melt and spoil in his refrigerator with the power down.

"Only cash!" he cries, defending his goods.

The power outage must be affecting people's ability to pay electronically, just like it blocked me from receiving any personal messages. Few people carry actual cash. So those desserts will all be wasted.

"Just a moment," I tell my group as I let A'nu slide off my hip. Once his taloned feet hit the metal floor, Cristobel immediately reaches out and takes his hand. After putting the lizard boy down, I pull the pulse rifle off my back and cradle it in my hands, casual as can be, except for the part where I'm holding a deadly weapon. "Is there a problem here?" I call out to the wolf-alien hoarding treats that won't do anyone any good once they've spoiled.

The crowd parts around him, leaving a clear path between me and the wolf-alien. He shifts uncomfortably at the sight of my rifle, even though I'm pointedly aiming at the ground. "No problem," he says. "Just protecting my property."

I look at my own little group surrounding me—three toddlers, a kid, and three adults plus me. "We could use some treats about now, right? That would lift our spirits in this trying time, wouldn't it?"

Still clinging to Jaimy's back, T'ni makes a tiny, cheerful, chirping sound. A'nu yanks his hand back from Cristobel and jumps up and down clapping, long tail swaying behind him, until the cat wrangles his hand back into hers.

Max nods solemnly. Too old and dignified to jump up and down clapping on cue, but still a kid and still desiring treats.

So, I step up to the food stall, look over what I can see of the menu in the hazard lights that throw a red-orange cast on everything. I pick a selection of treats that I know my kids will like—I know their tastes well enough to pick for them—and tell the wolf-alien what we want.

"Only cash," he insists again, but his voice wavers.

"You keep tabs for people." It's not a question. I don't actually care about the answer.

"Yes, sometimes, but..."

"Take my information, and if we're all still alive tomorrow, I'll come back to pay." I hiss the words, low and angry. He's making people more miserable than they have to be. "For now, I think a lot of people could use a nice cool dessert."

The wolf-alien looks at my rifle. Then he looks at the crowd surrounding us, the crowd that had been hounding him, sounding increasingly angry but that has now turned eerily quiet.

It really is eerily quiet. Sure, there are people arguing and calling to each other in the distance, but there's also a sound that's missing.

There's a low humming that I never noticed before, not really, because it happened all the time on the space station, and right now, it's just totally gone. It was the sound of air being pumped through filters and heat recyclers. A good sound. The sound of life. Like blood rushing through your own body, a sound so close to you that you don't hear it anymore. But when it's gone? You're dead, even if you don't know it yet.

And as long as we're all dead walking, we might as well be eating ice cream.

The wolf-alien harrumphs, gets out a pile of desserts that match my requests, and then types my name and credit ID number into his computer by hand. I wave my family up, and they each take the treats selected for them from the small counter—fruit-flavored ices for the s'rellick boys and me; peppermint ice for Max; and pastries for Jaimy and Cristobel. Jaimy's pastry is filled with a nut paste; Cristy's with thick cream.

After that, Kth steps forward, selects simple sweet ices for herself and Kalithee, and pays in the same way, by providing her information for possible future billing. Then the dam's broken, and as we leave, I see that the rest of the crowd follows in our footsteps, getting the same treatment from the now-subdued wolf-alien.

The frozen desserts won't be wasted. Whether the wolf-alien gets paid or not is a problem for a different day—a day with light and life support. For now, my group heads onward, sucking and licking and nibbling and slurping at their sweet treats as we go, moving much more slowly but also more happily. A little sugar lifts the spirit and loosens the hold of terror that was starting to settle into the pit of my stomach. I think it's doing the same for the others too.

As we walk, Maya—I mean, Max—tells Cristobel about his new name, and they decide he'd like to try cutting his hair short. Kth takes an interest in their conversation, intrigued by the idea that humans can simply change their gender presentation if they feel like it. Max, who's been studying up on history and likes showing off for adults, explains that this hasn't always been the case. Some human societies—like the one Max grew up in—are much more controlling.

Kth expresses sympathy, saying, "Our queen chooses our roles for us before we are born. Her nursemaids sing songs to us of who we'll become when we hatch from our eggs and emerge from our chrysalises."

I feel like I can hear a note of dissatisfaction in Kth's musical voice. Is this why she's the only Ll'th'th I've ever seen caring for a caterpillar? Has she broken with the societal role the queen picked for her? I wish I had time to ask, but while I've been trying to keep tabs on my group's conversation (because it's important to keep up on what my kids are thinking and feeling) I'm also trying to listen for any signs of danger in the darkness. We've passed several groups that look ready to break out into fights already. I don't want us taken by surprise.

Cristobel and Max lead the way, finding stairwells to use

instead of elevators and stopping to plug the briefcase-battery into doors that won't open for us.

Finally, we make it to the docking region of the ring. I can see *The Kanga's* berth in the darkness ahead of us. An especially dark patch between two other docked ships that are supplying their own light. Part of me wishes *The Kanga's* lights were on, ready to welcome us home, but most of me is glad that she's smart enough to play dead and avoid drawing attention while we're gone.

Almost home.

Almost safe.

Then I see a pair of Ll'th'th guards standing on either side of *The Kanga's* berth, almost invisible in the shadows except for the dimly glowing patterns on their wings. I stop walking and stare at them, trying to make out the details.

They're wearing armor over their fuzzy bodies and wielding weapons that look much fiercer than mine in their long, stick-like arms. In hand-to-hand combat, I feel like I could take a Ll'th'th or two down. I bet their limbs break easily. Though, honestly, I don't know how strong those stick-like arms are, and I definitely don't want to go up against their weapons—which look like full-on machine guns—with only a pulse rifle in my hands. Realistically, I don't want to go up against them at all, not while shepherding my family through a dying space station. Getting dragged into a physical fight is very different when you have toddlers to protect instead of just yourself.

Maybe my reaction here is too extreme. I don't know. But when you're on a sinking cruise liner, out on the middle of the ocean, without enough lifeboats for everyone, and you own a lifeboat... you get damned protective of it. And you don't want to see armed guards standing in your way of boarding it.

I wonder what the Ll'th'th soldiers want, but also, I don't want to know. I just want to get my family past them, back inside our home.

4

I lean toward Kth and ask, "What can you tell me about those guards?"

"They're soldier caste," Kth says, fluting softly. "Soldiers don't usually leave the inner ring. I know nothing else."

I hoped for more inside information, but I guess it's not fair to expect one random Ll'th'th to know what every other Ll'th'th on the station is up to, even if the same queen does sing in all their minds.

I gather my family together, tell them to wait for me, and then step toward the berth of my docked ship, rifle at the ready. However, I do my best to draw attention away from my rifle— swaggering a bit and keeping the muzzle low.

"Hello there," I call out, still several long paces from the dimly lit soldiers. "I notice you're standing in front of the berth to my ship. Can I help you with something?"

"Yes," the guard on the left sings. "You can come with us."

The guard on the right follows up with, "Our queen summons you."

Well, that's about the last sentence I ever expected to hear in any context whatsoever, let alone the middle of a blackout on a space station. A queen summoning me? Hah. Okay. I try to recover quickly for the sake of my confused family behind me. "Why?" I'm guessing that queens and soldiers don't like to be questioned about their motives, even if those titles are more biological than social. Or is it both? Something that's all mixed up together like gender in humans? Either way, if I'm going to question the motives of a queen, I figure it's best to keep my question simple.

"We are not authorized to say anything more," the guard on the left says. "However, we have brought a gift."

I like gifts, but I'm not really in the mood right now. Still, maybe it will hold a clue to what this is all about.

The guard on the left lowers xer machine gun—thank goodness; I'm super not comfortable with how these soldiers have been wielding such unnecessarily deadly, overkill weapons—and lets it dangle from straps, laying against xer long abdomen. Xe reaches into a pouch near xer thorax and removes a small pouch, which xe holds out to me in a talon.

Reluctantly, I step close enough to reach out and take it. The bundle is cloth and unfurls in my hands. Soft, silky. In fact, I think it must actually be some kind of silk. A silken scarf? Why would the queen of the Ll'th'th send two soldiers to my ship with a scarf for me?

Then I see the metal clasp on the scarf—small, oval, silvery... and sporting a horrifying visage, like a cameo painted of a s'rellick screaming in pain and torture. My stomach turns cold and nauseous.

I know the face painted on this metal. This s'rellick's name was Reeth, and he died aboard *The Kanga*. The scarabs that infected him and killed him by exploding out of his body immediately started trying to eat *The Kanga*, and she had to fly up out of the atmosphere to kill them.

Later, after we'd escaped from Hell Moon, Jaimy and I had cleaned up the debris left behind—all the dead carcasses of the tiny, deadly, baby scarabs. I'd thought Jaimy had disposed of them. I guess, maybe she did. Maybe she disposed of them by selling them over the station's computer systems, and some Ll'th'th artist turned this one into a piece of jewelry attached to a silken scarf for the queen.

And the queen sent it to me.

If this is a clue about what the queen wants from me, I want nothing to do with it. I want to get off of this station as fast as possible. I want to leave it behind and never look back.

And yet, I look around the docking quarter with its erratic pools of light where people have set up emergency lamps and where light spills out of the open airlocks of the docked ships, and I see scared people. People trying to survive. People hoping the tiny island of warmth and air that they live on out here in space isn't about to sink into the darkness and leave them to die.

I can't just get in *The Kanga* and fly away if there's any chance I could help save all the thousands of people who live here.

Sure, some of them will escape on their own ships—like my family on *The Kanga*. But not everyone has a ship of their own, and even if all the ships docked here loaded themselves up to the gills with refugees, not everyone would fit.

If Fathomscape Station falls, people die.

"Okay," I say, turning the horrifying gift over in my hands, feeling the silk move smoothly between my fingers. "I'll come with you, but I need to get my family settled first. Understood?"

I'd like to think I won't take 'no' for an answer, but the truth is: they have machine guns. And I have toddlers watching me. Toddlers who I'm responsible for. I don't have a lot of say here.

"Please move with the utmost quickness of time," the guard who handed me the gift says.

"Will do," I agree, waving my family forward toward the berth to our home.

I place my palm on a sensor beside the airlock door, and the door slides open as if I simply unlocked it. Of course, that's not the case. *The Kanga* recognized my palm print, but she was probably also scanning the area in front of her airlock, watching my interaction with the Ll'th'th soldiers this whole time. She chose to unlock the airlock for me.

It's a good feeling having a family member who has your back. It's an even better feeling when that family member is a self-sufficient spaceship.

I stay outside while the rest of my family—including the Ll'th'th parent and child A'nu has glommed onto—file past me into the airlock and the dim light inside. Since we're on the station, both inner and outer doors to the airlock could theoretically be open at the same time—there's atmosphere here—but the way my family piles up just inside the door suggests *The Kanga* is playing it safe and insisting on seeing who all enters the airlock before opening her inner door. I crowd inside with the others and even the dim light hurts my eyes, which have adjusted to the darkness everywhere outside.

The soldiers stay outside. That's good. They're not trying to insist on holding me at gunpoint until I come with them. That's very trusting of them. Maybe naive. I'm halfway tempted to get aboard and tell *The Kanga*, "Blast off, get us out of here, run, run, run!"

But I don't.

There's still all those innocent people aboard the station, right? So... I can't just run. Not if there's a chance they can be saved. Although, I'm not sure what difference I can make on that front.

"Hi Kanga," I say as the outer door finishes closing, locking the soldiers with their machine guns away from us.

"We have guests," *The Kanga* states blankly, her voice emerging from speakers in the walls. Her voice is never very emotive, but she sounds nonplussed to me. Or maybe I'm projecting.

"That's right," I say. "Kth and Kalithee here are friends of A'nu's. They've come to visit for a playdate, since the toddler playtime got cut short by all this—" I gesture vaguely around us, indicating the state of the station.

"Darkness," Cristobel provides.

"Power shortage," Jaimy says.

"Adventure!" Max offers enthusiastically. It's good to see the kids are still in good spirits. I think the frozen treats helped with that. Probably, also bringing friends home to visit, even if that has me a bit on edge—as well as *The Kanga*, based on the slowness with which she's getting around to opening the inner airlock door.

For the kids though, I guess this is a fun adventure.

Maybe Max's idea of fun has been permanently skewed by how his previous life came to such a sudden end on Hell Moon. (At least from his perspective; for the rest of the universe, it was a hundred years or more.)

Do I have a kid who's an adrenaline junky? I find myself thinking over all the books and video games May– I mean, Max —has been devouring lately, trying to figure out if there are any dark patterns I need to be watching for. But it's hard to think about something like that right now.

Or maybe it's easier to worry about something like that than to really face what's actually happening.

"Come on, Kanga," I say, getting impatient. "Let us in." Then looking at Kth, I add, "Kth, say 'hi' to our ship, okay? Her name's *The Kanga*, and she's a really good ship, but she gets kind of nervous around organic lifeforms she doesn't know yet."

There's a whole history behind that sentence—an entire crew of organic lifeforms that *The Kanga* was forced to murder in order to stop them from wiping her electronic brain clean, essentially killing her. That all happened before my family ever met *The Kanga*. But Kth doesn't need to know about that. *The Kanga's* personal, criminal history is private.

Kth is still holding Kalithee in her long, stick-like arms. All four of them. She extricates one arm and waves vaguely at the ceiling, "Hi Kanga, I'm Kth, and my littlest of ones is Kalithee." The caterpillar waves a whole row of tiny, stubby arms. It should be an adorable, cheerful gesture, but it just makes me shudder.

I don't like that kid, and it makes me feel really weird that I have such an instinctive prejudice against the one child who was being really nice to my reptilian sons. Am I jealous somehow? This is the first time either of them has made a friend outside the family, and maybe I've grown a little feral in our insularity over the last year, recovering from the traumas we all underwent on Hell Moon. Perhaps I feel threatened by the idea of their affections stretching beyond the limits of our family?

But no, that doesn't make sense. I've never been jealous like that before. I always loved when Gaby and Cristobel made friends when they were a mere pup and kitten. It's the sign of a healthy child who can make attachments among new people and other children they meet. It's a sign that I'm doing a good job as a parent that they feel safe enough to open up to new people and experiences.

Regardless, *The Kanga* relents and opens the inner airlock door, letting us all enter her for real. I expect bright light to spill through the door once it opens, but *The Kanga* has her interior lights set low, keeping her halls dim.

"Okay, let's see if we can get these kids set up playing," I say.

Jaimy entered the airlock first, holding one lizard toddler in each arm, so she exits first and heads down the hall toward the common room.

Cristobel and Max peel off in the other direction, toward their shared room, talking about possible haircuts and changes in clothing style. Kth and Kalithee follow Jaimy and the s'rellick babes toward the common room.

"I'll check in on you guys in a minute," I call after Jaimy. "Can you get some toys out and..."

I trail off as Jaimy calls over her shoulder at me. "Don't worry. I've got this."

"Great." That leaves me free to go to the bridge and speak with *The Kanga* privately for a few minutes.

As soon as I get to the bridge, I want to sit down in the my captain's chair and just... be. Be in my home, my safe place. But I have things to do, so instead, I punch the codes into the safe built into the wall at the back of the bridge, open it up, and start digging through the weapons there. I don't know if the soldiers will give me trouble about going to see their queen while armed, so I want to have more options available—more weapons hidden on me—than just the one knife and the very obvious rifle.

Basically, I load myself up with weapons, strapping them on every part of my body, hiding as many small ones as I can. The more weapons, the more of a chance that those guards miss one if they make me strip down. It reminds me of what Jaimy used to be like when I met her—covered in long, matted fur with grenades, first aid kits, and even a yoyo hidden in her mats.

I smile remembering that. I mean, it's a sad memory, but also, it shows how far she's come. It was an act of trust for her to let me shave her mats off and get her groomed properly for once, and it's been a wonderful sign for her improved mental health that she's been willing to keep her fur short and clean since then.

"Okay, Kanga," I say now that I have all the weapons I want arrayed in front of me and am simply busy trying to strap them on to various limbs. "What do you know about this blackout? Is the power likely to come back, or are we looking at a mass death event in a matter of hours?"

"I don't know," *The Kanga* replies, her voice's tone even but somehow tentative. "The official information coming from Fathomscape Station is extremely limited and... dodgy. I've been communicating with the other docked vessels, and some of them are considering creating a coalition to feed our energy back into the station to power up some of the more essential functions."

"Life support?" I ask, knowing that's probably the top priority.

"Yes, life support," *The Kanga* agrees. "However, I have withheld information about my own energy supplies and capabilities pending more information. I don't want to get roped into supplying power to a lost cause."

Those words are so cold. And yet so necessary.

If *The Kanga* spends all her energy on fruitlessly trying to help a failing station keep from dying, we could end up dying along with everyone else.

It's better a few people live than everyone dies.

I really don't want to head back out onto Fathomscape Station, even with all these weapons.

And yet, the chances are good that the problem is something fixable. Faulty wiring. A broken component. I don't know. But it's too early to bail on thousands of people. Even if I am scared. Even if I don't see how my skills could be useful to a moth queen in this situation.

"I've been asked by those guards at your entrance to go see the Ll'th'th queen on the inner ring," I state, standing up, shifting my weight and settling out my gear, making sure it all falls comfortably against me. "I don't know what she wants, but she sent me... a disturbing gift." I pull the scarf out of a pocket where I'd stashed it and hold it up where I'm sure one of *The*

Kanga's internal cameras can see it. "Do you know how the queen could have come by this?"

"I do not," *The Kanga* answers. Her synthesized voice reveals nothing of her feelings.

"This scarab shell is from Reeth. The s'rellick who died aboard you." I wait, but *The Kanga* says nothing to that. And then I ask the same question I've asked a thousand times since we got here: "One of the scarabs couldn't have survived when you exposed them to vacuum, could it? Stayed hidden somewhere in your walls or wiring or something and hitchhiked back here with us?"

"It is extremely unlikely," *The Kanga* answers. "But as I've told you many times before, I cannot claim it's impossible. Such a scarab would have had to manage to avoid crossing the path of any of my internal sensors and also avoided eating any part of me I would miss for weeks while we traveled back here. And then it would have had to escape to the station—again without triggering any of my internal sensors—where it would have had to avoid any serious detection for nine months while still feeding its own appetite for metal."

"Yeah, it's unlikely," I agree. But it's such a terrifying possibility, I can't let go of it. I probably never will.

Some day, I'll be a hundred year old woman, living on Fathomscape Station (which will have survived this hiccup in its operations as if it were nothing), and I'll still have nightmares about a baby scarab having survived and avoided detection for all that time, only to pop up and kill everyone I've ever loved.

I shudder.

Except, there's still the gift from the queen. A beautiful, rainbowy scarf... held together by a clasp that means death.

Maybe she just thought it was pretty?

Maybe she has no idea what significance it holds for me?

That has to be it.

I mean, how could she know?

No one knows about what happened on Hell Moon except for myself, *The Kanga*, Cristobel, Jaimy, and May– I mean, Max. Jaimy probably sold the metal shells from the dead scarabs for a little extra cash, and the queen—having gotten ahold of one —simply thought I'd find it a thoughtful, pretty present.

Although, that doesn't explain why she's summoning me to see her. But then, I suppose, I do have a record of successful mercenary missions. I've worked for a whole range of employers in my time, doing a whole array of jobs. Perhaps she has a job for me. Something nice and wholesome and unrelated to scarabs who eat metal and reproduce via crackling blue electricity.

Whatever it is, the fastest way to find out is to get myself back outside and let those soldiers lead me to their queen.

"You'll keep everything locked up tight while I'm gone?" I ask *The Kanga*.

"Of course," she agrees.

"No one on or off."

The Kanga doesn't reply to that. Our power hierarchy here isn't entirely clear. Mostly, we act like I'm the captain of this little crew, but then, *The Kanga's* a living ship and doesn't really need a captain. I'm also basically the group mom—but mom isn't a role with absolute power, especially when two of your horde of kids are completely grown.

"If everything goes to hell, and I'm not back," I insist, "I want you to take the others and run. Don't let Cristy and Jaimy abandon the little ones here and come looking for me. You don't want to end up raising a human pre-teen and two s'rellick toddlers on your own, do you?"

"It would be difficult for a spaceship to properly raise organic children on her own," *The Kanga* agrees noncommittally.

I see the loophole here and work to close it: "There's no reason the little ones should be going back out onto the station proper until the power outage is totally fixed and under control. That's why I can't have you letting either Jaimy or Cristobel or the whole group of them complete with the little ones leaving. They need you, but you need them too. You know it."

The Kanga was designed to have a crew. She'll never be happy as an empty shell, filled with empty organs that are meant to host organic creatures. We're her family just as much as she's our home.

Although, in this case, I'm almost asking her to be a prison.

"What about the visitors?" *The Kanga* asks pointedly.

"I'll leave that up to you." I don't really want them to become a permanent part of our family, but also, I'm not going to kick them off the ship to die. And either way, we're talking about a hypothetical situation that doesn't involve me: what should *The Kanga* do if I don't come back? I both profoundly care about what will happen to my kids if I die or otherwise fail to get back to them... and also am painfully aware that I wouldn't be around to know the difference.

"Very well, I will keep Jaimy, Cristobel, Max, A'nu, and T'ni aboard until your return. And you will return."

"That's certainly my plan," I agree, noticing that *The Kanga* has already adjusted to May– Max's new name. With her computer brain, she probably thinks faster than me and will never stumble over the change. She's just swapped one name out for another in some algorithmic subroutine. I'm a little jealous, but I'll live with the stumbling until my tongue catches up with my brain. Max will understand, as long as I'm clearly trying.

"Alright, I'm going to check on the others before going," I say, heading out of the bridge and down the hall toward Cristy and Max's room.

I'm never entirely sure when to say goodbye to *The Kanga*. When I leave the bridge and we stop directly having a conversation? As I'm leaving the airlock and am actually aboard her for the last few seconds? Or just not at all, because she's an electronic intelligence and can tell I'm leaving and doesn't need me to say goodbye to her every time I go? I mean, she can still contact me over my wrist computer after I've left, so it's not like stepping off her floors has to be the end of our contact if we want to keep talking. At least, that's usually true. Today is anyone's guess.

I get to Cristy and Max's room and find the older feline already cutting the younger human's hair. Bits of frizzy dark hair have fallen on the floor in a circle around the seated child. Cristy is using a simple pair of scissors, carefully trimming and clipping, shaping Max's thick hair into a pleasing shape.

"Looks good," I say, leaning casually against the frame of their open door.

"I have ideas for simple ways to alter some of Max's clothes too," Cristy says.

"That way I can keep wearing my favorite things, but look more like I want to look!" Max's smile beams. Whether this is a phase or who Max will be forever, it's making him very happy right now for us to take his self-image seriously. I feel good about that, and I feel even better about just how joyful his face looks right now. I like it when my kids are happy. Their joy and energy bolsters me against the scary things happening in the rest of the universe... like power outages and soldiers waiting on my doorstep and creepy gifts from queens.

"I've told *The Kanga* to keep you all aboard while I'm gone," I say.

Cristy's pointed ears twist to the side, showing her concern, but she doesn't argue. She can read between the lines. "Okay," she offers, reluctantly. "Don't be gone too long, and message once you know what this is all about."

That's right, I realize: Cristy hasn't seen the auspicious clasp on the silk scarf the soldiers gave me. That's why she's not more worried. I start to say something but then bite my tongue. It's better to leave it this way. She doesn't need to worry, not until I know more.

"I'm going to say goodbye to Jaimy and the boys—the little boys—now."

Cristy waves her paw that's holding the scissors at me in a sort of vague goodbye; Max mirrors the gesture with his own hand. They're both waving me away—too busy with the mundanity of changing Max's gender signifiers to worry about the blackout or what I'm up to. That's how it should be.

I head down the hall to the common area and find Jaimy and Kth sitting at the breakfast table while the little ones play around the wreckage of T'ni and A'nu's eggshells. We never cleared the shells away after the little lizards hatched out of them, and their remains have become a kind of play area and napping place for the little guys.

Right now, Kalithee is in the hollowed out center of A'nu's egg, while A'nu places and removes the broken dome of the egg on top of it like some kind of peekaboo game. T'ni is inside his own egg, hissing every time Kalithee emerges with her rows of stubby arms spread. His hissing is akin to human laughter. Giggling fits. My little lizard sons are so happy they're having giggling fits over playing with this little caterpillar.

I smile in spite of myself. I may not like the caterpillar—unfair though that might be—but I do like how my kids are getting along with her.

Maybe when I get back from whatever the Ll'th'th queen wants, Kth and I can have a nice long conversation about our kids and our lives and I can find out why I've never seen a Ll'th'th caring for a child on this ring before. Or if the play date is over and the power outage over by then, I can just talk to Jaimy and find out what she learns while I'm gone.

"Hey, Jaimy," I say, "I'm heading out now." I pat my sides and hips meaningfully, letting her know I'm properly armed, even if most of the weapons have been slipped under layers of fabric to hide them from prying eyes.

Jaimy nods, catching the meaning of my gesture. It's very important to her that I be properly armed. She's a good, protective dog.

"You'll take care of this—" I gesture at the room, the playing children, the adult guest, all of it. "—while I'm gone?"

"Not a problem," Jaimy says. "I was about to offer Kth some tea and juice and crackers for the little ones."

I wrinkle my nose. The juice is normal juice, but the crackers are made from dried, compressed Eridani gadflies. I find them horrid, although technically nutritious. The little s'rellicks love them. I bet Kalithee will too. "Good idea," I say. "I wish I could stay and chat..."

"But her sovereign singing highness calls in her dulcet tones for you," Kth sings. "We must all obey the call of the queen."

"Yes, exactly," I agree. Though, I don't feel as certain that I *must* obey someone else's queen. She's not my queen. "Such a pretty way to put it. Do you know—" I hesitate, unsure if I should ask this. I start over, differently: "The queen sent a gift for me, with the soldiers. Should I take one to her? Is that how it works?"

Kth reaches a talon above her head and smooths the feathery tendrils of her long, gracefully swooping antennae. "I am not knowing the ways of this," she finally says. "Her children—as I am—do not with the bringing of gifts. We are gifts enough in ourselves. Perhaps your presence is all of the gift her solicitous highness desires?"

"Perhaps," I agree. I don't especially want to try to scrounge up a gift for a moth queen. I have no idea what that would be—what does a moth queen need or value? My presence, I guess.

"Might I with the asking," Kth asks, "be told of what gift her generous highness sent for you?"

"A scarf," I say. "A silk scarf." I don't mention the clasp. I don't want to scare Jaimy, and Kth wouldn't understand its significance.

"Such beneficence," Kth intones.

"Indeed."

With that, the conversation between us adults seems to have reached a natural conclusion, so I head over to say goodbye to my little ones.

I kneel down beside the broken eggshells. "Hey kiddos," I say, holding my arms wide. Both boys crawl into my arms, nestling their scaly bodies against me. They're not the most physically affectionate children—that title would have gone to Gaby as a puppy; she was the cuddliest little kid ever. But they love me, and they're trained well to share in my expressions of affection. I think they like it. They seem to. I stroke A'nu's back with one hand, and with the other I turn T'ni's long, angular face toward me. His eyes shine like purple nebulas. "Be good for Aunty Jaimy while I'm gone, 'kay?"

T'ni makes a trilling sound in the back of his throat that reminds me of Cristobel's purring. A'nu butts his spade-shaped head against my shoulder.

"You're good kids."

And like that, the embrace is over: T'ni scuttles back into his eggshell, and A'nu clambers away to pick up the lid of his eggshell again—Kalithee is already waving her stubby little arms, impatiently waiting for him to get on with their game. They have playing to do. It was already generous that T'ni and A'nu spared a whole twenty seconds for the boring attentions of an adult.

With my goodbyes said—or unsaid but tacitly understood, as the case may be—it's time to leave. Time to see what this queen wants from me.

5

I step out of the airlock, leaving behind my safe bubble of warmth and power and family and safety. Outside, the air is noticeably stuffy and warm already. It's erratically dark, the darkness broken by individual areas where lights shine in through the ring's windows from exterior floodlights on docked ships or where people have rigged up lamps or strings of mood lights. But mostly, it's dark, so much darker than Fathomscape Station is supposed to be.

Tasting the mustiness of the air, already suffering from the algae filters being unpowered, I'm filled with an urge to turn right back around, head back into *The Kanga* and either stay there or at least dress myself in a spacesuit in case everything here really does go to hell.

But the soldiers have already seen me with their many-faceted eyes. The facets glitter in the erratic lighting like a diamond catching firelight. Their machine guns are lowered, and their limbs are spindly, but they could stop me if they wanted to. I've already made my choice. I made it when I was standing on the bridge and chose to outfit myself with guns and knives rather than to ask *The Kanga* to disembark and get us out of here, headed for places unknown.

Places that might be better. Might be worse. But wouldn't be the home where I've lived most of my life, the space station I've always returned to between jobs and missions that have taken me away. The place where I raised Cristobel. And Gaby.

This is my first chance to ever see the inner ring, even after decades of living here. Very few people who aren't Ll'th'th ever get invited there. And in spite of everything, I'm excited. I want to know what it's like, what it looks like inside the ring that hovers above my head, turning in synchrony with my home. What's behind those dark windows that usually glow in my sky?

"I'm ready," I say to the soldiers. "Lead the way."

One of them takes the lead; the other waits, standing still until I begin following the first one; then xe falls in step behind me.

I walk between them, watching the slight sway in the soldier's glowing wings ahead of me, staring at the pale pink and lime green patterns on those wings. Abstract curlicues and concentric circles that look a little like fake eyes glow back at me, ghostly but oddly cheerful in the dark. Even in darkness, the Ll'th'th's soft, fluttery wings are still faded candy apple green and cotton candy pink—the colors of a carnival late at night, full of treats and rides and delights.

The way the soldiers lead me takes us back through the docking quarter, the way I so recently came with my family. There's more noise now in the darkness—I hear scuffles and shouting. Angry voices and clanking sounds, like fights are breaking out or people are simply breaking things.

I'm glad *The Kanga* has a strong airlock. No one is getting in without her permission. It would take a blow torch and a lot of time for an intruder to cut their way in, and that would give *The Kanga* plenty of time to batten the hatches and fly away.

She'd come back for me.

If she has to leave before I get back to her, she'd come back for me.

She's come back for me before, under worse circumstances.

Besides, I still believe this will all get sorted out. Whatever ancient machinery broke, breaking down the entire power system, it'll get fixed. Spare parts will get pulled out of long-forgotten storage areas in tightly packed but mostly unused cargo bays, and the engineers who keep things running will do what they do. They'll get things running.

There are going to be a lot of bruised egos and hurt feelings in the coming days, beyond the actual injuries and property damage. When the lights come back on, Fathomscape Station is going to have to deal with the aftermath of panic and confusion. People will have to take long, hard looks at how they behaved, how their neighbors behaved, and whether they can trust each other anymore. How to rebuild that trust once its been broken.

I'm glad I don't have a stall in the market section like that sweets vendor. *The Kanga* is much better protected when the power goes out than any living or working space aboard the station proper. Everything in the world that I value—everything I need to protect—is safely locked in a private vehicle, mobile and ready to run.

The soldier ahead of me comes to the seam between this docking sector and the market quarter my family walked through earlier. Xe leads me (and the soldier following behind me) to the wall at the outer edge of the wide hall that makes up this common area of the middle ring. There are sliding doors, locked down like the ones that trapped us in the toddler play area earlier, but also gaping holes where doors have been forced open or, in some cases, torn completely aside and left, twisted on the floor.

Those doors are solid, heavy. Anyone who tore through

them must have been feeling desperate. I feel my heart rate rise; my breathing quicken.

"The elevating chambers are without the power of motion," the soldier ahead of me sings.

Of course, the elevators are down. That's not a surprise.

"There will be much trafficking of the feet to get to her highest of highnesses. Are you being prepared?"

"Sure," I say. "I can walk. I don't mind a few stairs."

The soldier leads the way, and I soon find myself spiraling up floor after floor of stairs. I said I don't mind, but in this close, warm air... I do. I'm huffing and puffing and putting my hands on my thighs as I force myself to lift my knees again and again, climbing up toward the inner ring. I find relief, occasionally, in the slight breeze from the soldiers' swaying wings ahead of and behind me. The breeze doesn't make the air any more oxygen rich, but it does cool my face. And that's something. I'll take it.

I've gone up these stairs before, but not in a while. This side of the middle ring has many layers of shorter floors, unlike the wide, open corridor with glass ceilings looking up on the inner ring where the playgrounds and markets are housed.

As we continue spiraling up the stairs, we pass doors— mostly sealed and locked—onto various residential levels. I used to live on one of these residential levels, back when I was a kid. Most of my friends did too. But these days, I stay mostly to the docking quarter. It's a different, more temporary way to live on a space station, keeping your own separate space with its own docking berth rather than piled in to one of the sets of quarters, just a few rooms of your own, all bunched together like a giant apartment building.

Today, I like the freedom of living on a spaceship, rather than on the space station proper. But I do wonder if I'm robbing my second generation of children of the chance to run around the corridors, meeting friends, just being a part of this big community. I have fond memories of being a kid in the residential level, and I have fond memories of Gaby and Cristobel being kids there.

And yet... if we used a battery pack to pry one of these doors open right now, what would we find on the other side? Are parents putting their children to bed early, hoping they'll fall asleep and not notice when the air gets too thick to breathe? Are they fighting with each other for resources? Squabbling over portable algae packs that could keep the air in a single set of quarters breathable for an extra day or week, as long as those quarters are sealed off from the common corridors?

Or are they just trapped inside their own quarters, unsure about what's happening outside, without a portable battery pack to free them and banging on their doors, waiting and hoping for help that may or may not come?

I'm glad the doors at every level of the stairs are sealed. I don't want to see down those halls. I don't want to see what it looks like to live through an extended blackout like this without any hope of escape.

Because yes, we're up to an hour or so of blackout now, and that's a dangerously long time without functional life support in deep space.

Even as I head deeper and deeper into the station, farther and farther away from my own escape hatch, I know: my children, my family are all safe on *The Kanga*, and they can get away from here, fly to a planet with breathable air or a different space station that isn't boiling slowly into its own heat death.

They won't die.

And that makes me feel free.

Finally I notice: climbing the stairs is getting easier. The gravity is getting lighter as we climb higher. A point on the inner ring doesn't have to spin as far as a similar point on the middle or outer rings to cover the same arc of the circle they inscribe while turning. Thus the centripetal force is lower as we get higher, meaning the simulated gravity is weaker.

Between the lighter gravity and the warm, thick, humid air, I'm starting to feel light headed. Starting to imagine moths on the inner ring flying around in zero gee. Is that why they chose the inner ring? Less gravity? More flying for the winged insect aliens. I guess that makes sense, or at least it seems to right now, but my brain's pretty addled.

I started my day dealing with toddlers, which is enough to addle a brain on its own, but I've followed that up with an emergency blackout, dealing with one of my kids switching gender, inviting a guest into my home, and now a lot of physical exertion in a situation filled with fear and uncertainty.

I wouldn't expect anyone to think straight under these circumstances. I sure hope the queen hasn't invited me to come see her expecting me to be clever, because I'm not at my cleverest right now.

And of course, when it comes to brute force, she already has her own soldiers... I watch the pink-and-green glowing wings ahead of me sway back and forth mesmerizingly as the Ll'th'th soldier steps up the stairs, taloned feet clacking against the metal steps.

The soldiers aren't intimidating in their own right with those cape-like wings and feathery antennae above disco-ball eyes, but their machine guns sure are.

If the queen doesn't need my cleverness nor brute force... all that's left is expertise, and I really don't like that idea. I'm not an expert on much, and I'm still telling myself—over and over again like a chant in the back of my head—that there's no way the scarabs from Hell Moon could have gotten here. They didn't have spaceships, and they couldn't have built themselves any. They'd eaten all the metal available on the moon to work with.

No, they were stuck.

Stuck, stuck, stuck. Dwindling to dust and grave ashes on that moon.

Ahead of me, the first soldier reaches the end of the stair-well—the very top—and stops beside the closed door. She speaks into a wrist computer much like mine, singing sounds that don't register as words for me. It must be the Ll'th'th's native language, rather than the Solanese that most of the disparate alien species on Fathomscape Station share. A moment later, the door slides open, and I see another pair of soldiers on the other side. This pair of soldiers waiting for us seems much less heavily armed. I guess that makes sense; they're on the other side of a heavy door that protects them from the great masses of foreign aliens who aren't part of their Ll'th'th hive.

Even though I'm about to enter a totally alien part of the space station—somewhere I've never been before, surrounded by aliens who have no connection to me—I feel my anxiety level go down a little as I step through the threshold from the middle ring, where I've lived for most of my life, into the space between rings.

I know I'm standing in a liminal space—mostly, I know because that door I just walked through like it was no big deal has been locked my whole life. Kids living in the residential levels we just passed by on the stairwell used to dare each other to come up here and try to hack the door's electronic lock. It was the door that station kids told each other had a monster on the other side.

I guess all of us kids were partly right... Soldiers standing guard are a kind of monster, just a very pedestrian kind. And I still have trouble seeing the Ll'th'th as anything but lovely and sweet with their pastel colors and soft-looking fuzz.

I know I'm standing in a liminal space, but it doesn't look or feel like anything special. No window; no lights except for the flashlights held by the soldiers who were waiting for us on the other side.

The two soldiers who fetched me from *The Kanga* continue

to flank me, stepping to either side of me now as we all face off with the new pair of soldiers. All four of them sing to each other in the language I don't know. It sounds like a fairy chorus, something you'd encounter in a deep dark wood in a fairy tale.

Finally, the guard who led my way up the stairs turns to me and sings in Solanese, "Forgiving us you must be, as we are needing to take your armaments away from your person and storing them in safety for while you are here."

"No," I say, simple and self-assured.

"We will the burden of your protection be very caring of for you."

"No," I repeat. "You asked me to come here, not the other way around. I have no desire to inflict damage on your ring, people, or queen, but I'm not disarming myself during this unexplained blackout and mysterious summoning."

"Forcing you we can be," the soldier who'd been following behind me says, lifting the nose of xer machine gun ever so slightly. It's pretty menacing, I have to admit.

But those machine guns will stay menacing, whether I'm armed or not. And I don't want to find myself stranded, far from *The Kanga*, needing weapons and without them.

"I can turn around and leave," I offer, "or you can keep your hands—" *Talons? Claws? Hands will do.* "—off me and my possessions. Your queen summoned me with a gift, remember? I'm a guest here. Show some appropriate hospitality."

The four Ll'th'th soldiers sing to each other in the foreign language for a while; one of them speaks into a wrist computer, and then an answer comes back in the same singing tones, crackling over the wrist computer's small speakers.

I wonder what they're being told. Will they be ordered to forcibly disarm me? How much of a fight am I willing to put up? Am I willing to get gunned down, right here between rings, because I won't give up my weapons? Was my bluster all a bluff?

How many of them could I gun down before their machine guns tear me apart? How many spindly arms could I break? Would the carapaces of their thick abdomens burst like a watermelon struck with a hammer?

Finally, the guard who's been leading me says, "Special dispensation for you has been acquired. Come."

Damn. All the violent visions filling my mind melt away, replaced by the cold sense that I have to continue onward, farther and farther from my home and family, putting more and more dangerous space to retread between us.

My disappointment shows me that I was hoping these soldiers would give up in the face of my stubbornness and send me back home. If they're willing to bring me before their queen armed to the teeth, she really does want something from me. From me specifically. And I don't like that at all.

There aren't a lot of things that I'm specifically qualified for, not a lot of things I'm an expert on...

Still armed but feeling strangely cowed, I follow the soldiers through an extensive airlock with several stages. Multiple heavy, armored doors need to be opened with portable battery packs; air fwooshes past us, being sucked in and out of the sequence of mostly dark rooms. I suspect the complicated series of locks is to secure the two separate rings from each other in case of a pandemic or any other kind of contamination. Although, as we step out through the final armored door, I'm hit by a blast of air that feels bright and invigorating, like it's higher in oxygen than I'm used to. It's also almost sweet at the back of my throat, smelling slightly of apples and cinnamon.

Maybe the Ll'th'th of the inner ring also keep the balance of gases in their air different than on the middle ring. Do they breathe better than we do? Is quality of air a signifier of social strata that I hadn't previously been aware of? I thought the algae filters worked the same everywhere, for everyone. But maybe there's something better than the algae filters I'm used to, something saved for queens and their many royal children.

As we all saw from the toddler playroom, the lights are off here too. There are small, dim hazard lights though, which we don't have running on the middle ring. So, while the lighting here is dim—just small red lights set into the floors and walls—the overall illumination is more regular here, much less erratic than the individualized emergency lighting that we passed by on our way through the middle ring.

It's a little frustrating to walk through a mysterious, exciting place I've never been before—somewhere that the kids on the middle ring used to make up stories about—but only be able to glimpse dim shadows, missing out on all the details.

I see curves and soft, flowing lines, nothing like all the right angles and straight edges on the middle ring. How are the lines here like that? The inner and middle rings would have been built at the same time, designed by the same engineers. The inner ring existed well before the Ll'th'th purchased it from the Fathomscape Station government, so it's not like it was designed for them.

And yet, everywhere the dim red hazard light falls, I see soft curves and gently bending lines. I narrow my eyes and peer into the darkness, trying to understand, trying to puzzle this mystery out. The curving lines move, slightly, swaying as we walk by. They're not metal. They're something attached to the metal architecture underneath. I reach a hand out, casually, and let my fingers trail across the closest wall with its gentle billowing. I'm nervous about what I'll feel, but the surface moves away as I touch it. So light, my touch pushes it away. Cloth. It's cloth. Silk, I think, based on the smoothness of the fibers. Like the scarf the queen sent me.

The interior of the inner ring has been clothed in silk curtains and sheets, hanging everywhere, attached at the ceilings and draping to the floor with a gentle bend caused by attaching at the middle to the walls. A metal corridor has been turned into a silken tube. I feel like I'm walking down the entrance to a spider's web, and my skin shivers everywhere. I can feel the goose pimples rise on my arms and neck as I picture the Ll'th'th queen as a spider at the center of this web, waiting to eat me alive, or at least wrap me in silks, mummifying me and trapping me away from my escape and my family.

And yet, as we reach the end of the corridor and the space opens into a wide, broad throughway like the market quarter on the middle ring, I can't help but be delighted by the sight before my eyes:

The Ll'th'th here are flying. Okay, maybe not really flying, but they glide from one silken drapery to another, using their softly glowing, cape-like wings to let themselves drift gently through the lower gravity.

I want to spread my arms and join them, but I don't have wings. I don't have a cape. I have a bunch of heavy, concealed weapons weighing me down. I don't regret that. But I do wish I could jump into the air and sail across it the way the Ll'th'th do.

Watching the glowing figures flutter through the wide hall ahead of me, I'm struck by how light their bodies must be. I wasn't wrong when I assessed them as unthreatening. There's simply no way they could float like that—even with their wide, decorated, glowing wings—if their bodies weren't built out of lighter stuff than mine, Cristobel's, and Jaimy's.

I try to imagine Jaimy flying, and the image is preposterous. Her bulky canine body suspended between delicate, cape-like wings? Hah. Then my brain shifts the image—as it often does —and Jaimy becomes Gaby in my mind's eye. The image isn't funny anymore. My lost daughter looks like an angel to me when I imagine her soaring on gentle wings above me. She was always gentle. And fun-loving. She'd have loved to fly. She would have loved seeing this.

A beautiful butterfly puppy.

Then I picture Cristobel and Max and the little lizards with wings, swooping and swishing through the air all together... and I start wondering: is the richer air here, combined with the stuffy air while climbing all those stairs, staring to make me woozy?

I take a deep breath, hold it a moment, and then let it go slowly. I need to hold myself together. I don't know what I'm about to face, but it's not going to be what I fear most. The chances against the scarabs having come here somehow are astronomical—even if someone had been foolish enough to follow our tracks to Hell Moon, the scarabs would have killed them and eaten their ship before they could have gotten back here.

We barely got away. Once infected, each of our team members who'd been impregnated by them died within a day, leaving hungry, mindless babies in their place, eating any metal they could get their serrated mandibles on.

My skin itches at the thought of those baby scarabs, and I scratch at my arm, my hip, my belly. I'm remembering Tyler now—Jaimy's old guardian. It terrifies me, the way the scarabs hid under Tyler's skin, growing and eating him from the inside out. Death hiding under his own skin.

We don't always know what's inside us, not until it comes out.

I shudder.

Then the soldier in front of me says, "Be keeping yourself close now. No matter the armaments we left on you, they won't help if the monsters get to you." ·

My blood runs cold, and I say, mechanically, "The monsters?"

But the soldier doesn't elaborate.

"What do you mean, 'the monsters'?" I repeat, more urgently.

Still no response. Instead, the other soldier adds, "And avoid the ghosts."

I stop, turn, stare in the direction we came from and see what I had missed before: yes, the Ll'th'th wings glow naturally in pale pink, green, violet, butter yellow, and other shades. But they also glow supernaturally—blue and ghostly. Not all of them. Not most of them. Just a few, here and there. But those ones aren't a mix of colors like the others; they're monochrome, with all their swirling patterns in only pale blue.

I close my eyes while standing there, blocking out all the glowy flying Ll'th'th around us, all the red hazard lights, all the soft curves of silk. Everything I can see. I make it all go dark. I need to think.

Ghosts and monsters.

The guards said 'ghosts' and 'monsters.'

I don't know how, but they're here.

The scarabs are here. There's no other explanation for those words and the sight I've just seen. None at all. How did I miss it? How did I fail to see that some of the Ll'th'th shimmered translucently? I could see right through them, right through to the darkness behind.

And yet, somehow, as my deepest nightmare becomes real, my legs are frozen. I'm standing in place with my eyes closed, and I'm not running for my life.

6

If the guards had told me about the ghosts and monsters before we left *The Kanga*, I would have turned right around and flown away. No question. I would have gotten myself and my family out of here, away from a doomed station.

But I'm here now. On the inner ring.

I grit my teeth, open my eyes, and look down at my wrist computer. Messages still aren't going through reliably. I want to tell Cristobel and Jaimy to get *The Kanga* out of here, undocked and safely surrounded by vacuum—tell them to put a barrier between them and this contaminated space station.

But realistically, if the contamination is here on the inner ring—which it must be, based on those ghosts—the scarabs are unlikely to get all the way down to the middle ring, let alone *The Kanga's* berth in the docking quarter, before I can finish seeing the queen and get myself back home to them. We can all leave together. That will be better.

I send a cryptic message to *The Kanga*, Cristobel, and Jaimy to get themselves out of here RIGHT NOW anyway. Maybe it'll go through. Part of me hopes it does, because I want my family safe. But part of me is terrified that it'll go through, and I'll get abandoned here.

Or even that it'll go through and my family will decide to ignore it and risk their own safety to save me. The idea of that makes me furious with them and also feels like a relief in my mind. I don't want to die alone, without them.

There are so many possibilities right now, and so few of them are good.

I don't want to die here. I don't want to die at all. And most of all—I scratch at my arms, my side, my shoulder—I don't want those scarabs to touch me with their sparking blue energy that can fill my body with their tumorous babies.

It takes all the resolve I have in my body, but I turn back around, back in the direction of the queen, and step close to the soldiers like they asked. "Let's get this over with, quickly," I snap.

The leading soldier curls and uncurls xer proboscis in a way that feels like an acknowledgment, a sort of alien nod, and then xe starts leading the way again.

The soldiers flank me closely now, close enough that their wings brush against me. I feel the soft, dusky scales of one of their wings whisper across the back of my hand, and it's oddly reassuring. The soldiers might not be physically tough, but they're wielding machine guns, and I'm important to them. I'm important to their queen, their mother, so I'm important to them. It feels weirdly nice—kind of special—to have guards protecting me.

It feels less nice to be heading towards some kind of throne room or whatever on a space station ring infested by the monsters from my literal nightmares. As we walk now, I find myself glancing at the shadows, eyes darting rapidly toward anything that looks too dark or shady. I'm afraid I'll see red eyes set in impassive obsidian faces. I'm afraid of scarabs hiding in the shadows.

I'm also afraid of scarabs eating through the station's walls, breaching the hull of the inner ring, and blasting us all into a vacuum. It could happen at any moment. Life here could end in an instant. But then, I guess that's always true, even if it feels more pressing right now.

I have to keep reminding myself that a station like this is protected against that kind of breach—heavily protected. There are bulkheads between sections and reinforced segmentations and extra layers of hull shielding and... I don't really know. I've never studied space station engineering, but I know a place like this doesn't survive for generations—or even just a few years—without redundancies and protections. Space is harsh; mistakes happen. Space stations are ready for them. They have to be.

I tell myself that, over and over again, but it doesn't stop the fear from curdling in my stomach, roaring with acid that claws at the back of my throat.

Finally we pass through a series of draping curtains which flutter aside gently at our touch, and on the far side, I see *her*.

The queen is seated laconically on a throne, surrounded by computer displays and attended by dozens of her daughters. She's larger than the other Ll'th'th—probably three times my height and bulk if she actually stood up instead of lazing sideways. Of course, that's not accounting for her extra long and feathery antennae or her widespread wings that drape away from her like the train on a wedding dress. She's massive and would struggle with the elevators and stairwells here. It seems strange to me that she's chosen to live in this metal box rather than on a planet with a sky wide enough for those giant, colorful wings.

But then, I suppose, it doesn't look like she moves around a lot. She's practically wired into some of the computers around here.

As I stand and stare at her, I'm surprised by how little security we passed on our way. Just the guards at the seam between rings. If I were facing a human monarch—or even just a big time politician—I would expect a lot more layers of security before entering their presence. But then, I guess, things are different when everyone who lives on your entire sector of the space station is your own daughter, son, or some other gender of offspring.

There are guards posted here, standing around the edges of this large throne room, but they're not armed liked the soldiers who have been escorting me. They're lightly armed, ceremonially armed even, with multi-bladed metal weapons, shaped a little like sickles if six sickles were glued together in a row. I wouldn't want those crescent blades slicing into me, but also, I have plenty of ranged weapons hidden on my body, so I'm not overly worried about them. They're pretty though. I wouldn't mind having one hanging on the wall of my room on *The Kanga* as a decoration, as long as I hung it high enough that the little s'rellicks couldn't get it.

Well, if I have to fight my way out of here—which I really hope I don't have to do, as I still have guards wielding machine guns on either side of me—I'll try to see if I can grab myself a souvenir.

The Ll'th'th directly attending to the queen are smaller than the soldiers or the workers I'm used to on the middle ring. Their wings are stunted, looking like they haven't fully grown in yet. I don't know if they're a younger stage of the life cycle or a different bio-social class of Ll'th'th. Also, I don't really care right now, because my curiosity about this species has mostly been burned away by the rage boiling through my whole body. I feel like I could float away on rage alone.

I don't wait for the soldiers who've escorted me to announce me. I charge ahead of them, insolent and aggressive. I plant my feet firmly with a wide fighting stance and shout at this queen, "How did you find the moon? And why did you go there?"

If she wants my help, she can answer my questions first.

"A bold little child you are being," the queen sings. All the Ll'th'th around her stop—just briefly—as she starts singing. They shiver a little as she speaks, like the voice of their queen and mother makes them cold. Or maybe fills them with such pleasure it can't be contained and has to be allowed to wash over them.

I bristle at being called a child, but I suppose she's surrounded by children. Everyone who isn't a queen, mother to an entire society, is a mere child to her.

Joke's on her. I do have an entire society. Our family may be small, but it's good, and I'm its queen.

"Not a child," I say, "and if you want me to answer your questions or try to help you, then you'll answer mine. Fair play."

"Fair play," the queen repeats in a sing-song way. "Bold and demanding. A survivor."

"Yes," I agree. "I'm a survivor, and I'm guessing that's why you brought me here. You want to know how I survived on a planet with the monsters who are attacking your ring and still lived long enough to escape and stand here today."

"Yes," the queen agrees. Her attendants brush her feathery antennae. They droop aesthetically like the branches of a willow tree. Other attendants move along the edges of her draping wings, seeming to massage the colorful tissue with their four upper talon-hands. "The Dor'ecki are strong. Good warriors, I thought. Sharp mandibles; metal-hard carapace. Good defenders."

I laugh derisively, but don't otherwise dignify the queen's statement with a response.

There's nothing quite like getting a grizzly bear as a pet to guard you... only to be mauled to death by a grizzly bear. I just wish I—and thousands of other innocent people—didn't live in the other half of the shack that this queen brought a grizzly bear into. She's a fool. Such a fool. This is why I had *The Kanga* working to track down any mentions of that solar system on the Fathomscape computer systems and simply erase them from official files. She wrote a computer virus specifically for the purpose. And we logged the most boring mission reports possible everywhere they'd been required. Mind-numbing, extremely detailed reports about absolutely nothing. The kind of reports that would make readers cross their eyes and fall asleep reading.

We did everything we could to draw attention away from Hell Moon and avoid the monstrous scarabs there from coming to the attention of someone as foolish and powerful as this queen.

So what went wrong?

The queen offers nothing more, so I press my point.

"You didn't answer my second question: how did you know about the scarabs—the Dor'ecki, as you called them?"

"Beautiful poem," the queen sings. Her attendants shudder and sigh at the sound of her words. "Read a beautiful poem of loss and tragedy."

My eyes narrow, and I can feel my brow furrowing. I'm trying to figure out what she could mean as consternation mixes up my insides. "What are you talking about?"

"Paintings and poetic captions, beautiful art. Traced back to the berth of your shuttle."

With a coldness inside that fights the rising heat on this space station like a fever fighting for control of my body, I suddenly understand what must have happened.

Jaimy is an artist, and while she would never have gone against our plans to keep Hell Moon secret... she must have been processing her way through the loss of Tyler with her art. And posting it on support boards.

For a flash of a moment, I was afraid that Maya—I mean, Max—had been indiscrete, being the youngest and most endemically online of us all. But poems and art? That's Jaimy.

I'm angry... but also, I can't blame her. Tyler was her rescuer, her supporter, and her only friend from the time she'd been abandoned by the family that raised her until she joined the family I've been building. He was a horrible, annoying, petty, foolish man... but he'd been important to her. His tragic death was a huge loss for her, much as Gaby's death has been a huge loss for me and Cristobel.

I can't blame Jaimy for processing her pain through art. I can't even blame her for sharing cryptically captioned pieces of art. I can, however, blame this queen.

Even so, I can't blame all the generations of sisters, innocent children of hers, who will die for her mistake if this station goes down.

Nor the miasma of aliens living on the middle and outer rings who haven't been involved at all.

"What can I do to help you?" I ask, though the words grate against my own ears. I don't want to say them.

"Understanding, I seek." The queen shifts her abdomen, twisting at the right wing which drapes over her almost like a blanket. Or a tapestry.

I wonder whether the scarabs born from moths will feature the full complexity of their mother-moth's wing patterns on their own metal wings. I wonder if the answer to that question is already here, eating away at the station.

The scarabs born from Reeth and Tyler bore twisted, horrified and horrifying visions of the s'rellick and human man painted into the metal of their wings. I reach into my pocket and feel the tiny, oblong piece of metal the queen gifted me, still attached to its silk scarf.

Have scarabs already been born from Ll'th'th bodies? Bursting out of their abdomens and thoraxes, possibly tearing through their delicate, candy-colored wings?

How far on the path to destruction have we already walked?

I don't think this queen, no matter the size of her army, can stop the scarabs if they're here.

And they're here.

I haven't seen them, but I've seen the ghosts left behind when those they impregnate are killed before coming to fruition. And the queen herself admits to bringing monsters here.

It's too late to save us. To save everyone. But maybe some can be saved.

"I'll tell you what I know," I say, "but quickly, and only if you share your own information in return and then get me back to my ship as fast as possible. I want an armed escort again, just like the one that brought me here." If I find myself fighting scarabs, I want disposable bodies I can throw between them and me. That may sound brutal, but so's this whole situation.

"Bargaining," the queen sings. "How human. Well-met. Deal-made." Then the queen gestures with her long, stick-like arm toward a Ll'th'th soldier armed with one of the multiple-bladed sickle weapons. "Sh'n'nai will represent for me."

The soldier, Sh'n'nai, steps toward me and bows so low that xer feathery antennae brush against the metal floor.

The air grows so thick with the smell of cinnamon and, oddly, burnt sugar that I feel like I could choke on it.

"Go with Sh'n'nai. Tell all. Hear all. Share. Exchange. Plan salvation." The queen gestures dismissively at the guard and me with three of her arms. With those words, apparently, she's done with us. She's delegated the problem, and that's all there is to it for her. She's an administrator. She doesn't get her many hands dirty with solving the problems she's caused.

"Plan salvation," I grumble to myself as Sh'n'nai leads me away from the queen. "Is *that* all."

I follow Sh'n'nai away from the queen's throne room through a series of twisty corridors that eventually lead to an area that looks like a cross between a prison and a mad scientist's laboratory, complete with a row of holding cells filled with nightmares. My nightmares.

After all my nightmares and day terrors, fearing this exact moment when I would face the scarabs again, I'm surprised by how I react. Which is not at all. There they are—lined up in transparent holding cells, built from plastic or force fields or something else the scarabs can't eat. So not metal.

Their red eyes gleam like the dying embers of a fire; their obsidian faces writhe with wriggling mouth parts at the base of those serrated mandibles. Their taloned feet clack on the floor, shuffling restlessly, and occasionally, one spreads the metal wings on its back, splitting its painted carapace down the middle. There are five big ones with different patterns drawn on their wings—twisted, agonized figures I don't recognize. But there are also five smaller ones—three with Tyler's twisted visage etched into the pattern on their metal wings; two with Reeth's, like the baby dead one in my pocket.

"Where did they come from?" I ask, needing to know whether those scarabs with Reeth's reptilian face on them hitchhiked here with me.

"Her highest of highness's brave and loyal expedition to the moon of empty deserts brought all back. Elders captured underground in ruins; juveniles captured on surface by remains of wrecked vessel," Sh'n'nai answers.

So, I guess some of the scarabs that gestated in Reeth's body escaped to the surface of Hell Moon before *The Kanga* jetted up to outer space to blast them out, and they found their way over to the wrecked vessel where Tyler died. Big scarab family reunion.

"Okay," I say, a little relieved that this isn't my fault. Which won't save any lives here, but I guess, I still care that they won't be quite as much on my own conscience. "Now quit wasting my time with this 'highest of highnesses' nonsense and get to the point—these Dor'ecki are trapped. So, what's the deal? Did some get out?"

"New ones born," Sh'n'nai answers, xer voice low and haunting like a mournful flute solo.

New ones born. I know what that means. Exactly what that means. It means death. It means living people dying, spectacularly, as their bodies explode from the cruel baby scarabs crawling around like tumors under their skin.

"How many Ll'th'th died... *that way?*" I ask.

"Three before queen executes rest of crew. Rest of crew rises from dead—ghosts, impossible," Sh'n'nai's voice has stayed quiet. Deeply mournful. I wonder if xe had close friends among the crew. Xe collects xerself and adds, "Brave heroes. Sacrifice for queen, very honorable."

Very foolish, I think. But it's not the crew's fault they were sent on a fool's errand, and no one deserves to die that way. I watched it happen to Tyler. It was brutal.

"They died here?" I ask. "On the station?" I'm running calculations in my head—wondering how the infected, impregnated Ll'th'th lived long enough to get here; multiplying three Ll'th'th bodies by the number of scarab-tumor-babies each body could support; and simply trying to imagine how deranged the queen had to be to send her own children on this mission in the first place.

I guess, when you have as many children as she does, they start to look expendable. Disposable.

"Yes," Sh'n'nai answers. "Died on station. Small Dor'ecki escaped before we could effect containment."

So that's what's eating the station. Three Ll'th'th's worth of baby scarabs. Three dozen or so little beetle-shaped metal-munching tumors.

"How long ago?" I ask. I need to know how long they've been eating for; how long they've had to grow... and critically, whether they're old enough to begin infecting more people and multiplying exponentially.

"Five days," Sh'n'nai answers, and I think, maybe, maybe we're okay. It took five days for the baby scarabs to cause this much damage, and there's only about three-dozen of them probably. There might be time to contain this problem. They're not old enough to infect anyone yet. They can't be. Then Sh'n'nai shatters my hopes: "But small Dor'ecki... they eat controls on holding cells."

My blood runs cold. "What do you mean?"

"Release more than half Dor'ecki prisoners before disappear into bowels of station." Xe gestures down the hall of prison cells holding my nightmares inside them and I see something even worse than my literal nightmares: empty cells.

Empty cells that should have been full.

"How many escaped?" I ask. "And were they juveniles or elders?"

"Ten juvenile. Twelve elders."

That's potentially twenty-two more Ll'th'th infected and ready to explode into more baby scarabs at any moment. If they were s'rellick or human hosts, it would have happened already. However, from the fact that the queen's mission made it home from Hell Moon, I can only assume that Ll'th'th hosts take longer to incubate scarabs than humans or s'rellick do. That's not such a surprising idea. S'rellick already take substantially longer from infection to explosion than humans do. A fact that nearly killed my whole family back on Hell Moon when several infected s'rellick were in deep denial about their impending doom and thus hell-bent on sharing it with those of us who weren't infected.

Also, it's a lot more free scarabs eating. Eating metal. Eating the hull and guts of Fathomscape Station.

"Holy hell," I say. "This whole damn station is going down, and there's not a damn thing anyone can do about it." Is that true? Do I know that's true? I feel it in my bones, but a feeling isn't a fact, no matter how much it *feels* like one.

"Juveniles do not infect," Sh'n'nai says.

"What?"

"Juveniles act different."

The Ll'th'th guard and I stare at each other. I think xe wants me to tell xer that a difference of ten fewer infections will save the station. I can't do that. I don't believe it. We're all going to hell. Hell Moon. Hell Station. Hell Universe, if we're not careful. These things are a cancer upon reality.

At this point, I just need to get out of here alive, escape with my family, and hope the whole station blows to bits before any scarabs can escape and infect another station or world.

But first, if I want to get out of here safely, I need to fulfill my end of the bargain I made with this foolhardy moth queen. So, I start talking fast.

I tell the story of my own mission to Hell Moon, trying to divorce the words coming out of my mouth from the rest of me. I don't need to get dragged down in a lot of emotions right now. I don't need to re-experience Tyler's death, Reeth's death, Ahn's-si's death at my hand, S'rissa's suicide, or Gaby's...

No, I can't let myself fall down this hole. I say the words to Sh'n'-nai, skipping past the worst details, and holding a wall around my heart while I hear my own voice describe that doomed mission.

When I've finished, Sh'n'nai says, "That... is not as helpful as our highest highness hoped."

"No kidding," I say. "I'm not a scientist or any sort of expert. Just a survivor. Just a fighter. And the only way I know to win a fight against these scarabs—the Dor'ecki—is to avoid fighting in the first place. There's a reason I left them to rot down there on Hell Moon and did my damned best to erase every record I could of that whole star system even existing. If I could have hidden the whole thing inside a black hole, I would have."

"That would have been best," Sh'n'nai agrees bitterly.

"Now can I get out of here?" I ask. "'Cause I think you guys need to get to work on abandoning the station, and I need to do the same, right quick."

"Her highest highness will not abandon," Sh'n'nai flutes. I can see the gears working in xer alien head. Xe's trying to figure out if xe needs to remain loyal; if xe has to go down with xer queen and the station.

Or if maybe there's another way out.

I don't want to... I don't want to become some sort of Noah's Ark for drowning, disaffected moth soldiers and workers, but... The top priority right now is getting out of here, getting myself back to *The Kanga*, so I say, "I have a ship. Get me back to it, and I'll bring you along."

Sh'n'nai hesitates. I think xe's seriously considering my offer.

The scarabs in their cells continue shuffling their talons, clacking their mandibles, and shifting their metal wings, making cacophonous, monstrous sounds. It's not quiet in here. While Sh'n'nai continues to think, I say, "You should kill them. If you lose backup power to this room, if the little Dor'ecki come back and start eating away at controls again, you don't want more adults to escape."

"We try," Sh'n'nai says. "Know not how to kill, except by exposing to uninfected Ll'th'th... and allowing to infect."

"And then executing the newly infected individual, who would rise as yet another ghost," I add. "Yeah, that's not a great solution." Though it might be better than allowing the scarabs to escape, infect unsuspecting Ll'th'th, and then end up with even more of the hungry baby-tumor-scarabs. I don't say that though. I say something else, something that might give this hesitant guard a bright silver line of hope, something to hold onto hard enough to distract xer into letting me go: "There must be something that's poisonous to them. Some kind of gas? Some kind of biological agent?"

Honestly, it troubles me that this prison-slash-laboratory isn't filled with scientists working on this problem right now. But then, I suppose the queen wasn't looking for a science project. Just a bunch of work-horse soldiers she could tame. To bad for her they turned out to be less like wild horses and more like rabid bears.

Too bad for all of us. The clock is ticking, and if Sh'n'nai doesn't send me on my way in a matter of moments, it'll be time to start forcing my way out of here.

My hands slip into position—one on the hilt of a dagger, and the other on the butt of a gun. Then I see something that stops me. I can't stop looking at the scarabs in their cells, almost like if I keep looking at them, they can't escape, can't attack me. It's irrational. I know that. But still, it means I finally notice something new: there are eggs on the floor of the cells of the juveniles. I didn't notice them before, because they're positioned protectively behind the scarabs in those cells.

Unwittingly, I start to step forward, to see more clearly, but that causes the closest juvenile—a scarab with Tyler's twisted visage painted on its wings—to rear up. I back away instead.

I would like to imagine that the scarab has reared up out of sheer aggression, but against my wishes, I know more about these scarabs than that. I experienced a vision back on Hell Moon when Ahn'ssi's ghost walked through me. She showed me their civilization, as it should have been, back on their original world, and I know these horrendous monsters care for their young, in their own way. Not the tumor-baby-scarabs so much; those are allowed to live or die in a sort of free-for-all of Darwinian survival-of-the-fittest.

But the other half of their life cycle? The half I haven't seen in person yet?

The scarabs worship the maggot half of their life cycle.

When the scarabs have enough resources, they lay eggs and carefully tend them, rearing the maggots that hatch from them with tender love. There's no other word for the emotion they feel toward the maggots. It's love, as much as I love my own children. As much as I loved Gaby.

"They've laid eggs," I say to Sh'n'nai, who seems to still be pondering my offer to take xer away with me combined with my contradictory follow-up demand that xe start experimenting with how to kill these scarabs immediately.

Hey, I never claimed to be consistent. I never claimed anything to these moths, and they dragged me here anyway. Jokes on them: just because I survived tangling with the Dor'ecki before doesn't mean I know anything helpful to them. Anything other than, *"run, run now."*

"What can you tell me about the eggs?" I ask, a war waging inside myself, because I need to get out of here... but the more I know, maybe the safer my family will be. Or maybe... I'm just curious. Maybe it's just the horrible human compulsion to stare at a train wreck while it happens. Because this is the worst train wreck I've ever seen in my life. It's so bad, I'll be lucky to survive it.

And yet, I can't stop staring at those filmy white, almost translucent eggs with their weird crenellations, almost like they'd been piped out of a frosting bag with a metal tip shaped like a starburst. They're almost beautiful. They look a little like giant dumplings. And while they're a natural part of the scarabs' life cycle, I almost feel bad for them, almost protective of them myself. Because I know that the creatures that hatch out of scarab eggs look nothing like the scarabs—they have long tentacle-like limbs and pale soft skin. They're more like humans than scarabs, which is why Tyler and Reeth and all the rest of us look good baby receptacles to the scarabs.

It doesn't make sense to want to save the maggots from their own scarab parents, but I just find their life cycle so viscerally horrifying, I almost want to.

I guess, maybe that's not so crazy. There was a time way back in the dark ages of human history when unwanted pregnancies were a real problem, and people were forced to carry unwanted babies—and sometimes even unviable fetuses—to term. Horrifying. Barbaric. So, maybe, its not insane to look at those eggs, imagine the maggots that will hatch from them, and feel sorry for them that they'll be expected to become receptacles for tumor-scarab-babies. Maybe they want birth control and safe abortion options like humans have now too.

But they're not gonna get it. They're probably not even gonna get to hatch. Not on this station, not with their kin eating up all the metal, munching their way towards chewing holes in the hull.

I pull myself together. Sh'n'nai has been telling me what xe knows about the eggs which mostly adds up to a whole lot of nothing. "Look, I think we're done here. Do you want to come with me or not?"

Sh'n'nai begins to answer, and that's when the lights go out. Again. These lights were only emergency lights in the first place, dim and awkwardly placed, but they made it so I could see. Now I'm in the dark with only a thin layer of plastic—or maybe a force field that's gone down who knows—between me and a lot of scarabs, some of whom are old enough to impregnate me.

Blue light crackles, lighting up one of the cells. That's more than enough of an invitation for me: I pull my handiest gun and begin firing.

Usually firing into the dark isn't a good policy.

But we left the realm of good policies a long time ago in this room.

The sound the bullets make flying through the room—because the gun I've pulled is projectile based, not sonic or laser—tells me that the cells are open. Sh'n'nai is probably moments from being impregnated; I will be too if I don't get away. So, I keep firing as I back away.

I strain to hear anything useful past the deafening booms of my own gun, but my ears just aren't that good. They can't recover from the sound of gunshot fast enough to hear anything of a reasonable volume before the next shot. Not with me firing this fast.

I hope I haven't accidentally shot Sh'n'nai... then I think, hell, xe's probably better off dying from a bullet now than facing any of the other options coming up.

When I get far enough back into the corridors that brought us to this hellhole prison, I turn and run, fast as my legs will carry me.

7

As I run, I chant my children's names under my breath to keep me focused, keep me from panicking. *Cristobel, Jaimy, Max, A'nu, T'ni, Gaby.* I know Gaby's gone, but her name's on that list forever anyway. I still have my gun in my hand, but I'm not brandishing it about anymore. I'm hoping the guards with the machine guns will have more important things to worry about than me when I get to them.

Running through the dark, I keep bouncing against walls, catching on the silk the Ll'th'th have hung there and having to shake it off my shoulders, careful not to tangle my feet in it. Better to slow down and not trip than to tangle myself up and end up rolling on the floor.

I make it back to the throne room—I'd love to have avoided it, but I don't know the floor plan here, so retreading my steps is the only certain way back out—and the queen is singing orders to her guards in her sing-song language. There are more lights here, so I can see she's raised herself from her throne, though wires and tubes still trail away from her body, suggesting she's not going far. Not easily, anyway

Like I hoped, the Ll'th'th here seem too busy to care about me.

Then the queen turns her glittering, disco ball-like eyes my way. Not literally, I mean, she probably has 360-degree, full surround vision with those things, but somehow, I can tell she's changed her focus toward me. Maybe it's the tilt of her feathery antennae. She sings something in her alien language, and several of the guards in the room turn my way. I think they can see way better than I can in the dark. And some of them still wield machine guns. No one needs machine guns on a space station. Even now, they're not going to save these people from the doom they've brought down on themselves. But they do make me hesitate.

I don't point my gun at anyone, but I lift it in a way that makes sure the guards are aware I'm holding it. For a moment, I think about punishing this reckless queen for what she's done. I could raise my gun and shoot her right between her glittery eyes for how she's doomed thousands of people to their deaths. I could do it in a heartbeat. My hands are fast.

But if I do that, I'd be throwing my own life away. Her devoted, machine gun-toting children would kill me for sure.

A piece of petty revenge isn't worth trading my whole life for. So, instead I argue.

"We made a deal," I say. "I honored my half. I told Sh'n'nai everything I know. I don't think it was very useful, but then I'm not the one who thought dragging me here was a good idea. So, what about you? Are you gonna honor your half of the deal? Are you honorable? Or do you not have to be, since everyone around you is a curly-tongued, glitter-eyed sycophant?"

Maybe insulting the queen's children isn't the right move here. I don't know. The air feels tight, and I'm not thinking straight. I'm surrounded by guns, and there are monsters coming fast on my heels. But it's worth taking a moment to try to talk my way out of this throne room rather than shooting my

way out. I don't want a machine gun pelting bullets into my
back as I try to run.

The queen sings again, and the guards stop approaching
me.

I press my point: "I'm useless to you. Let me go." I think
she's thinking about dragging me along with her like some kind
of stupid good luck charm. But I am no one's rabbit foot.

"Tell you what, you don't even have to send guards with me.
I'll let you out of that part of the deal. *Just get out of my way and
let me go.*" I really would have liked a pair of guards flanking me
back to *The Kanga*, but now is not the time to quibble over
details. In moments, the loose scarabs will be here, infecting
people, and I don't want to get caught in the crossfire as these
zealots protect their mother-queen. I don't want to be mown in
half by a rain of machine gun bullets.

Or worse than that—get infected.

The moment for bargaining is over; ghostly blue light
sparkles in the hall behind me. "They're coming," I say. "If they
touch you, you're dead. Good luck, foolish queen." And with
that, I start moving again, backing away from the monster-
infested hall, keeping my gun ready. I know I'm backing toward
machine guns, but I also know they have bigger problems to
deal with than me.

The moment machine gun fire rends the air into the thun-
dering soundscape of a war zone, I drop all pretenses of
caution, turn away from the disaster that's happening in front
of me and run, run, run.

I run through dark, winding corridors, still catching on the
silk hung everywhere. It looked pretty at first, the way it
smoothed out all the sharp metal corners, but now every time
one of the silk hangings catches against my arm or foot, I just
feel like a fly about to get caught in a spider's web: stuck,
wrapped up, mummified, trapped where the big scary bug can
come eat me at its leisure.

And I can still hear gunfire behind me.

I get back out to one of the broader, wider halls, and I see the various glowing Ll'th'th fluttering about—some alive, some Dor'ecki-infused ghosts. There's a frantic quality to their movements now, like they're listening to their queen sing a death song. They probably are. Or might be.

What must it be like to have your queen's death—your mother's death—sing real-time inside your mind?

I keep running, trying to retrace my steps, trying to remember how those guards led me. But it's dark; the corridors are obscured and unfamiliar; and I'm scared. It's hard to do anything well when you're scared. I jump at every shadow, every flicker of light. And there are a lot of shadows and flickers, even though none of them so far have been the lethal blue light of a scarab intent on impregnation. But soon enough, I know: I'm lost. I have no idea how to get back down to the middle ring where my family is waiting for me.

Running will just get me more lost. So I slow my feet. I sheathe my knife; though I'm unwilling to loosen my vise grip on my gun. But one free hand is enough to fiddle with my wrist computer, hoping against hope that messages are getting through again.

No luck.

Nothing from Cristobel, Jaimy, or *The Kanga*. I don't even know if my last message to them got through. Regardless, I dash off another. Telling them I'm on my way. Telling them to wait. Telling them to get out of here as fast as they can. I don't even know what kind of contradictory nonsense is pouring out of my brain, through my fingertips, and into the ether to find and confuse my family on the other side. I think I'm halfway writing a plea for help and halfway writing my goodbye letter.

I wrap it up without taking the time to make it make sense. I don't have time to spare for something like that. Or brainpower.

Then I try to access station maps. I find one that might be of some help, but it freezes up after only a corner of it has loaded. Damnit. And then the emergency lights all around start to flash —a warning sign that things are about to get worse, and since nothing will load on my wrist computer, I don't even know how. Just worse, generically. Possibly less life support. Hey, maybe it's even just circuit in the lights themselves causing them to flash. I've never been in an emergency on this space station that's lasted this long before, so I don't even know the protocols. In school, we learned the earlier stages of emergency protocols, but I guess, the people in charge of setting the curriculum figured that if the station truly went down—all the way down, game over—that there wasn't anything us civilians could do about it. So, hey, no point in scaring the schoolkids by making them think about it.

I'm panting from the thick, hot air by now, and I know that's only going to get worse if I can get back to the middle ring. The air quality was degrading faster there. And if the lights are strobing here, turning everything into a flashing nightmare scene, the emergency lights are probably entirely gone there.

All out war is more likely to break out between the citizens on the middle ring. At least here on the inner ring, everyone's one big family, all Ll'th'th, all on the same side, all siblings... except for me. And most of them don't know or care that I'm here. So, I'm a lot less likely to get caught in the middle of a last gasp gang war. Because whatever happens here, it'll be guided by the singing of their mother-queen in their minds. It'll probably stay peaceful.

Whereas, if it was bad in the middle ring an hour ago with people on the edge of breaking into fights over spoiling desserts, who knows how bad it is by now.

With sadness, I realize, I'm not even trying to get back to the middle ring, where I've lived most of my life, where I grew up, where I raised my kids. I'm probably never going to see it again. Because my best chance here doesn't lay in that direction. My best chance at survival—and it's not a good one—lays directly on the other side of the hull.

I need an airlock. And while I don't know the layout of the inner ring, I do know basic maintenance and safety rules for this station. And those rules dictate: there must be an airlock nearby.

I don't know. Maybe this is a bad plan, and I'm just a coward who can't handle the idea of seeing my childhood home shuddering through its death throes. Or maybe the air is getting so thick that I've correctly assessed that getting back to the middle ring—where I just know, *I know*, it'll be worse—is a recipe for ending up lying on the metal ground, halfway home to *The Kanga*, gasping like a fish, with no chance of rescue unless I let some of my kids risk coming out to get me. And I can't let them risk that.

At least, with an airlock, if I can get a message out, it'll be *The Kanga* herself who tries to rescue me, while everyone else stays safely aboard her. I mean, yeah, I know that the kind of airlocks I'll find around here aren't going to be the right size for The Kanga to dock with them. They're going to be simple, small access locks for letting maintenance workers get to the outside of the station. But hey, if *The Kanga* positions herself just right, and I blast myself into space at just the right time... well, we can play a horrifying game of catch with my body in a zero gee vacuum. That sounds like a good idea right? No?

Well, right now, I'm not sure my head is clear enough to recognize a good idea if it comes up and punches me in the face. So, I'll just have to stick with this idea. It's what I've got. And yeah, I am kicking myself for not taking the extra few minutes to put on my spacesuit before letting those Ll'th'th guards drag me away from my home.

Well, my personal home.

This whole place is my home. This whole space station. And that's why I felt comfortable enough—foolish enough, safe enough, I don't know—to walk around in here with only a few flimsy, permeable layers of cloth protecting me from the elements. Or lack of elements, which is probably a more accurate description of the vacuum outside.

If I survive this ordeal, I swear to myself, I'll sleep in a spacesuit for the rest of my life. I'll wear it to bed instead of pajamas.

Sure enough, after a few more twists and turns, I find myself a corridor right up against the outer hull with an airlock in it. Bonus points: the emergency lights aren't flashing here, which is much better for my sanity. Those flashing lights were making me really jumpy.

Better yet, the airlock is completely unguarded. Nobody's around. Why would there be? It's just a simple maintenance lock, no good for evacuation unless you have a ship specifically coming for you, and the problems on the station right now are all crawling around *inside*, not out there on the hull waiting for maintenance workers to fix them.

Unfortunately, all the air is in here with the problems. I look at my wrist computer and am not surprised when there's still no messages for me. I send another message to *The Kanga*, copying Cristobel and Jaimy on it, anyway.

Eventually it will get through.

Eventually.

All I have to do is wait, which is fine, just as long as *The Kanga* gets my message before a scarab finds me here, dallying uselessly beside an airlock, or the inner ring runs out of air, or the scarabs eat something too essential to the station's integrity and this whole little bubble of a world pops in a series of cascading explosions...

Damn, this *is* a bad plan.

But surely, surely, as people start dying, the digital traffic will die down too, and I'll be able to get a message through to *The Kanga* about where I am.

Goddamn, what a morbid thought.

And yet, as I stand in this backwater hallway, away from the crowds of Ll'th'th—ghosts and otherwise—coming and going, away from any flashing emergency lights, away from most of the pressing, visceral reminders of the disaster my whole world is undergoing, it's eerily easy to forget. To pretend it's a normal day, and I'm just bored, standing here and waiting.

Well, while I'm waiting for people to die—and trying like crazy not to picture all the people I've ever interacted with laying about gasping to death—I should make sure I know how to operate this inner ring airlock, so I'll be ready to blast my body into space when the time comes. It probably works just like middle ring airlocks, but it's worth checking before I get even more lightheaded from oxygen depletion. Or carbon dioxide poisoning. Whatever's happening to make the air so shallow I'm starting to gasp like a fish myself. So, I examine the control panel—it looks perfectly normal. Then I check the supply closet next to the airlock, which usually stores a few emergency tools, mostly locked down so that only maintenance workers with the appropriate codes can get them out.

But this time... *jackpot.*

There are three whole-ass spacesuits hanging in there, not locked down or anything. Just hanging. Like some sort of gift from the fairies, especially to me. I feel like I've fallen down a rabbit hole and found a whole tea party waiting for me.

I guess this is a difference between the inner ring and the middle ring—if everybody's family, everybody share's, so nobody's stealing. They can just store spacesuits next to the airlock where they'll actually be needed, instead of insisting that every maintenance worker own and lug around their own suit at all times.

I yank one of the suits out greedily. Of course, it's shaped for a Ll'th'th body—six spindly limbs, a narrow thorax, huge abdomen, and weird thin, flat sheaths for their wings. Even so, I can't believe my luck. Cannot believe it. If I'd pushed myself to face my fears and get back to the middle ring, pressing forward against my growing concerns, I'd be so much worse off.

Now, I just need to find a way to cram my body into this weird spacesuit, use its built in jetpack, and fly myself home.

8

Holding the Ll'th'th spacesuit up against myself like some high school kid examining a prom dress that's way out of their league expense-wise, I can see there's no chance I'm squeezing my legs into any of those six spindly sleeves. Ll'th'th simply have narrower, longer limbs than mine. If I bunch up the bottom-most set of legs though, I can probably squeeze my arms into them. That's not ideal, since they end in booties instead of gloves—designed for foot talons instead of hand talons. Still, it's better than nothing. The helmet is big enough for my head, thank goodness, but that leaves my torso and legs.

I perversely wish for the time, supplies, and skills necessary to cut this misshapen garment into pieces and sew it back together in an entirely different, much more human shape. (It would be so much easier to just wish for a human spacesuit... but hey, I'm getting woozy here.)

I guess this is another reason the Ll'th'th can store spacesuits next to their airlocks, and the rest of us don't. The rest of us, in the middle ring, come in a much wider variety of shapes and sizes, being a whole bunch of different species.

Still, I'm holding a spacesuit in my hands, and that's better than I was doing a few minutes ago. I am going to find a way to make this work.

But first... I check my wrist computer again. Dammit, still no reception. If I have to rely on getting a message through to *The Kanga*, I am going to die here. So, I'd better make this spacesuit work.

I stop thinking and start doing, shoving parts of myself into the spacesuit's opening, willy-nilly. Head and right arm, then a leg, which really, really doesn't fit. It doesn't take long until I'm completely tangled, trip over a dangling sleeve, and thump down onto the floor on my butt, unable to catch myself with any sort of saving grace, because both arms are still mixed up inside some part of the suit.

I feel like an idiot who's gotten my head stuck up inside a turtleneck shirt, unable to figure out how to get out. Though to be fair, at least a turtleneck shirt—as much as I don't like them —is designed to fit my actual body.

This suit is not.

But it's my salvation. It's my lifeline. I need to make it work. So, I extricate myself from the tangled folds of fabric and hold the whole thing out in front of myself again.

The problem was that I was too eager. And I didn't stop to think. Always stop to think when you're trying to save your own life in the depths of outer space. No matter how much it feels like you don't have time to stop and think, the alternative is invariably worse.

Looking at the shape I have to work with, I can see my only option is going to be shoving my legs into the baggy part of the suit designed to hold a Ll'th'th's long abdomen. It'll be like hopping about inside a sleeping bag, which is gonna feel silly as hell, but it's the only feasible choice I have.

Given my new plan, realistically, I want to be traveling around inside the space station as little as possible once I'm folded up like a piece of origami inside this ridiculous space-suit. So, I open up the airlock's inner door and get inside.

Thank the heavens, the airlock door works without a portable battery-pack, unlike so many of the fickle doors between that toddler play area and *The Kanga's* berth. I guess keeping airlock doors running during an emergency is a higher priority. Also, less of a risk contagion-wise, in case that's the kind of emergency. Which, I suppose, in this case it actually is... but metal doors won't stop hell-monsters who eat metal.

I close the airlock door behind me, trying not to think about the fact that I've just exited Fathomscape Station for the last time. There will be time to mourn later, when I've made damn sure I'm not one of the people who needs to be mourned.

Safely ensconced in the airlock, I dash off a quick, final message to The Kanga, Cristobel, and Jaimy, letting them know about my plan. Letting them know that they need to be on the lookout for me. Then I set my wrist computer up to broadcast the message again, every few minutes, until I tell it otherwise. Operating my wrist computer is going to get a whole lot harder once I'm inside this Ll'th'th spacesuit, so I want to get my communication out of the way now. I don't want to rely on the suit's internal computer system or my ability to operate it after stuffing myself into the thing like it's a much-too-small child's sleeping bag.

With that out of the way, I step my feet into the baggy abdomen part of the spacesuit. I have to wiggle my legs around, bending my knees awkwardly, because my legs are longer than a Ll'th'th abdomen. So, I end up twisted over on my side, on the floor, because I can't seem to balance on my knees with my legs folded in half. Next I put the helmet on with its weird bimodal shape designed to accommodate moth heads that are mostly two giant disco-ball like eyes. A panel between the two halves of the helmet runs right down the middle of my face, blocking much of my view. I'm going to be relying a lot on peripheral vision.

Finally with my head and legs suited up, I start working on shoving one arm after the other into the tight, constricting leg-sleeves of the suit. I feel like I'm trying to find the least inconvenient way to wear a straightjacket. Spoiler: there isn't one. A straightjacket's still a straightjacket, even if it's the only thing standing between you and asphyxiation.

Still, I'll take it. I'll take this weird cross between a child's sleeping bag and a straightjacket, and I'll ride it all the way home.

With the overly long, overly thin leg-sleeves bunched tightly up around my arms, squeezing uncomfortably, I manage to operate the booties over my hands well enough to get the whole suit properly zipped up and airtight. Awesome. Now I just need to blast myself into outer space, fly around like some sort of weird bug, and get home.

I turn on the air inside the suit I'm wearing—I can't think of it as 'my' suit when it fits this horrendously badly—and my mind immediately starts to clear, along with the sickly sweet cinnamon-apple smell that had gotten thick enough to chew on. The new air smells antiseptically plain. My ears pop; my lungs expand in relief. I hadn't realized just how much they'd started to ache from gasping at the bad air.

Then the clearing in my mind overshoots: it goes from being a nice, wide, empty sky—a good clean slate, ready for me to write my thoughts on it—to a glaringly bright, cluttered jumble of puffy pastel clouds and vividly oversaturated rainbows. I'm saying the higher level of oxygen is making me giddy, and I have to stifle a giggle. Now is no time for a laughing fit.

And yet, suddenly, everything feels hilarious. My nightmares have come true, and my world is shutting down. That's funny, isn't it? In a dark way?

I mean, I'm kind of kneeling on my knees inside a stolen

spacesuit designed to be worn by a moth—it has four empty, extra arms dangling in front of me and sheaths for wings that I don't have hanging off my back like a cape. If the wing-sheathes had been designed differently, I might have been able to stuff my legs into them, instead of having to fold my legs up in the abdomen, but no, the moths kept the sheathe fabric too rigid for it to stretch out that way. I don't know if that was a lack of foresight—because clearly, whatever moth engineer designed this thing should have foreseen the situation I'm stuck in right now—of if stiffer fabric actually serves a purpose by protecting their delicate wings somehow. Either way, it feels utterly ridiculous to be squeezed up so tight in a spacesuit that's dangling extra parts all over the place around me.

I'm absolutely losing it here. And I can't afford to lose it yet. I can lose it when I get back to *The Kanga*, and my whole family is flying away from this mess. A sob-laugh escapes my throat as I tense my jaw, trying to clamp down all the emotions threatening to bubble up. Usually, I hold myself together under pressure better than this. But usually, I haven't just gone from oxygen-starved to oxygen-flooded. I should have tried to adjust the air controls on this suit before putting it on. Too late now. And yeah, that is just insane. You don't want to be in a spacesuit where you can't adjust the controls, but...

The alternative is staying aboard Fathomscape Station, waiting to die with everyone else here.

Because they're all gonna die.

And I don't want to be one of them.

I push myself up from the floor, just enough that I can reach over and slap the controls for the airlock outer door. I don't bother venting the air back into the station first. I know that's wasteful, but hell, it's not like it would buy a meaningful difference in anyone's life. Probably. Though, now, I'm picturing a pair of Ll'th'th taking one final moment to say the things to each other that had never seemed worth saying aloud before, singing their final song of love and goodbye...

And oh well, they just won't get to, because the outer door opens, and the air inside the lock with me blasts out, blasting me out with it, giving me a good head start on flying out of here.

Of course, the blasting air hit my twisted up body unevenly, so I'm tumbling knees over head over knees, which wouldn't matter in deep space, but right here next to the space station? It means I can see the giant shape of Fathomscape Station spinning dizzily around me. I mean, it's not spinning. I am. But same difference in outer space.

I must still be giddy from the extra oxygen, because it feels abso-crazy-lutely hilarious to me that I'm floating through outer space—a big, wide, empty space—and I'm all squeezed up like some bully shoved me into a locker. Well, more like shoving me into a locker after wrapping a bunch of duct tape around me. This suit is so tight my arms and legs are going to start falling asleep on me very soon. I can feel the tingling in my toes and fingertips already.

Step one: I need to stop spinning before my stomach revolts. It's already getting queasy, and closing my eyes doesn't help because as much as orientation is relative in space, the centripetal motion of spinning is still very real. Fortunately, even with my hands inside booties meant for feet, I'm able to work the simple jetpack controllers built onto the front of the spacesuit's torso.

So I start blasting short pulses of the spacesuit's jetpack—first one side which makes things worse, then the other. Apparently I'm so dizzy from all this spinning, I couldn't even tell which way I was going. But after a few more short pulses, I get my spin slowed down to a lazy turn.

Fathomscape Station now drifts lazily from one side of my bimodal, peripheral-centric vision to the other, then disappears, then shows up again on the other side. It's a slow enough turn that I can think again. I can get a good view of the whole station as it scrolls by. I've seen it from the outside before—obviously, since I've both lived here my whole life and also made various mercenary excursions to other solar systems when hired—and other than the darkened windows that should be glittering with bright, tiny views of station life, like a length of old movie film, it looks just the same.

For all their munching on the station's innards, it's not like the scarabs have taken a big bite out of one of the wheels. There are no tooth marks out here. No sign of big explosions. The station is still three concentric wheels, spinning through the endless night of deep space. In fact, the only weird thing going on from out here—again, other than the darkened windows—is the way that a lot of the spaceships are behaving. Usually, there are bunches and bunches of spaceships of all different sizes and styles latched onto the docking portions of the rings, like little mechanical pups suckling at their big mechanical, toroidal mom. But not now.

No, most of the spaceships have undocked and removed themselves to a safe distance—not far, just far enough that no one inside can try to break through their airlocks and over-burden them with hopeful-survivors.

For all of humanity's progress, for all that we made it out to the stars and made friends and alliances with whole other alien species, at some level, we're still just hapless passengers sinking into the ocean on the Titanic, and all the ships are lifeboats, trying not to get overturned. My high school history teacher would probably be thrilled that I still remember that arcane, useless ancient Earth history lesson... assuming they're still alive. Which if they are, they won't be for long. Not enough lifeboats.

Okay, I need to get to *The Kanga* before I lose all feeling in my legs and hands, because operating the jetpack on this suit is just going to get harder as my fingers get more and more numb from restricted blood flow.

I punch the jetpack thrusters a few times and get myself moving toward a better vantage point. A little more distance from the station makes it possible to see the middle ring more clearly. I scan my eyes over it—trying not to get too frustrated by the opaque band blocking out the middle of my vision. Turning my head back and forth, trying to follow the curving line of the middle ring's outer edge, I finally spot *The Kanga*. She's still docked. They're still waiting for me. I cringe inside. I mean, yes, obviously, I'm thrilled that my kids love me enough that they haven't given up on me coming back home alive. But also, I'm out here now, and there's just nothing good that comes from them being docked. Also, it does mean that they haven't received my messages. They're not going to be expecting me.

I guess it'll come as a big surprise when I literally knock on *The Kanga's* outer hull, asking them to let me in.

Now that I have my goal in my sights, I push down hard on the jetpack thrusters. I don't want to overdo it too much and smash myself into *The Kanga* like a bug on a windshield—god, I really do feel like some sort of weird bug with my knees all folded up like this and all these extra spacesuit limbs and wings extruding from me. But also, I want to get home fast. I want to be inside a spaceship and have Cristobel and Jaimy help peel this spacesuit off of me. I want to move on to the part of my life where I can afford to feel all the emotions creeping in all around the edges. I want to be safe so I can fall apart and cry.

That's when I see the first explosion happen. It's small—vacuum dampens down explosions right quick—but there was definitely the red, hungry color of fire involved. It happened fast, almost so fast I think I must have imagined it, but then there's a chain reaction effect, and I see the explosions creep along the far curve of the inner ring, toward one of the spokes connecting it to the middle ring. Crumpled, broken pieces of hull are left behind. Now it does look like someone's been chewing on Fathomscape Station—not like someone took out a big bite, but more like a giant space beast has been using the triple-torus as a chew toy, munging it up along one side. The explosions reach closer to *The Kanga* than I'd like, and sure enough, it's closer than *The Kanga* likes too, because now I see her disembark.

Well, good for my kids. They're rescuing themselves and leaving me behind. I feel a sickly mix of fierce pride at their wise choice and cold rejection at their abandonment. Combined with the queasy feeling from all the spinning earlier, it's not a good mix. But I don't have to hold on much longer. *The Kanga* is growing in view; I'm getting close. Her metal body is built a little like a frog—central bulk with bunched up extensions on the sides that look like strong legs ready to jump. Of course, they don't jump. They fold space, letting *The Kanga* slide through the universe like a needle jumping from one side of a piece of fabric to another. That's what we're going to be doing real soon...

Real soon...

As soon as I'm back on board...

CLOSE, closer, *crash*. The metal side of *The Kanga's* hull fills all but the very edges of my peripheral vision now, and my whole body aches from crashing into her. They probably heard my impact on the inside, so I guess I don't need to knock after all.

Yes, that's right, I got caught up in daydreaming about the end of civilization as I know it and misjudged and failed to slow myself down enough to stop myself from slamming right into the side of *The Kanga*. And in turn, her immovable bulk knocked the air right out of me. Fortunately, this joke of a spacesuit kept hold of my lost air for me, and maybe when my lungs stop aching I can manage to start breathing normally again. Right now, I'm kind of wheeze-panting. It's not pleasant.

I turn myself around to get another look at the station. The explosions have stopped, but the damage would take years of work to fix, even assuming some kind of miracle scenario where the people onboard are still alive by tomorrow. The darkness behind those windows is oppressive; the parts of the station where the windows flicker red with fire behind them are worse.

I'm watching a hundred or more years of civilization crash down in real time. I thought I'd grow old here. I thought I'd be an old woman, walking through the market quarter, watching new generations of children playing in the playgrounds.

Now I don't know what my future looks like. It's narrowed down to a pinpoint—my kids and *The Kanga*, clustered behind me right now, at least physically. But when I look forward to the future, that's all I can see. I can't see anything around us. Just us, trying to find somewhere else worth living in this big, hostile universe. This disaster has destroyed everything in my periphery and all that's left is tunnel vision. My loved ones, surrounded by infinite darkness. I must protect them. But first, they need to let me back inside.

"Come on, guys, where are you?" My voice cracks as I say the words to myself.

I tear my eyes away from the darkened, crunched toroid that used to be my home. It's time to start crawling my way along *The Kanga's* hull. I need to get to the airlock.

Part of me wishes that—now I'm out of Fathomscape Station and safe from the disaster happening there—the whole place would just blow up in a single, spectacular explosion. If this disaster could hurry up and finish unfolding, I could finish grieving everything that's being lost sooner.

Start the grief sooner, end the grief sooner.

But right now, I'm trapped in the middle of it, still

wondering if any piece of the station can be saved, how many people will escape, what kind of refugee camp we might all manage to set up in the asteroids...

I don't want to be in the middle of a disaster; I want to be at the end of it.

Yet, from another angle, that's just saying I wish everyone would hurry up and die faster so I can move on. And that's just horrible.

Rebuilding is better than surviving, not only because it means you're reaching forward, towards improving your life instead of just scraping by during an absolute calamity... but also, quite simply, because it means you've already survived.

I hate to admit it, but right now, I still don't know if my family and I are going to survive.

Why haven't they sent someone out through the airlock to rescue me yet? I should be showing up in their scans. Cristobel or Jaimy should be coming out here to help me. I don't know how much longer I'll still have use of my hands. Both of my legs have already stopped tingling, and not in the good way. No, they've passed all the way through to the other side of numbness, fallen so far asleep that it's become a coma.

9

I awake with a start. Nothing feels real. Then a horrible beeping rends my ears, and I know what happened: I passed out, floating right outside of The Kanga, right outside of my home, and yet also a million miles away if I can't get inside. And the low oxygen level warning in my borrowed spacesuit awoke me.

It keeps beeping, making it hard to think, but I can't operate this cocoon restraining and sustaining me well enough to turn the alarm off.

How long have I been floating out here?

At least, *The Kanga* is still right beside me. I didn't float away; my family didn't fly away, unaware that I'm right here.

Though, they do seem to be unaware. If they knew, they'd bring me inside... right?

Unless, something horrible has gone wrong aboard my ship...

God, that beeping. It's driving me insane.

Okay, I can only think between the blasted screeches of the alarm, but I *need* to think. As far as I know, there's nothing wrong with this spacesuit, so it should have had at least several hours of oxygen. Which means several hours have passed, and either my family simply hasn't received the messages I sent them—telling them to look for me out here—or they're incapacitated somehow and couldn't do anything to help me.

I may need to help them.

I'm not in any kind of condition to help anyone. My arms and legs and basically all of me feels numb and unreal. My head is pounding, and of course, it's pounding out of rhythm with the beeping, so the sound and the pressure in my skull fight with each other like two songs of clashing genres played at the same time.

Okay, step one: get inside. Step two: who the hell knows; I'll figure it out when I get there. Step one is hard enough for now. I couldn't work this spacesuit properly before my whole body went numb, and now, I'm fumbling with fingers I can't feel properly just to operate the jets. Regardless, I manage to awkwardly maneuver myself around *The Kanga* with minimal ramming of myself into her hull. I'd like to imagine that my family inside can hear me bashing into *The Kanga's* outer skin and will come rescue me, saving me from this undignified scrambling, but she's a spaceship. Her walls are too thick and reinforced for my squishy body smashing into her to make a sound loud enough to be noticed on the inside.

Eventually, I find my way to the outer doors of the main airlock and use my completely numb hand to beat at the control panel. It's not an effective way to work the control panel —that would require pushing specific buttons in a specific order, and that's well beyond my numb fingers inside their ill-fitting booties. It is, however, an effective way to harass *The Kanga* and make her aware that something weird is going on right outside her airlock. After that, it's up to her.

My plans never get far beyond "step one," do they? I guess I never was much of a planner.

Come on, Kanga. You have to be feeling all this noise in the form of your buttons being randomly mashed.

Yes! The outer airlock door slides open. My spaceship heard me. Never mind that she didn't notice me slowly dying only inches away from her outer skin for the last few hours... I'll have time to mull over and be hurt by that later. I know it's not her fault—her outer skin isn't designed for the kind of sensitivity it would have taken to notice me. But it still hurts.

Everything hurts.

I jet into the airlock, and immediately my stomach lurches, my body falls, slamming against the floor, jarring my shoulder and sending shooting pain all down my side. I forgot that the artificial gravity would be on as soon as I glided into the open airlock. Damned gravity. Now I'm squashed on the floor, unable to do much of anything but flop about in this ridiculous straight-jacket cocoon mummying me.

"Kanga! I'm in! Dammit, close the outer door!" Can she hear me? I'm still surrounded by vacuum, still mummied. The sound won't carry. She wasn't picking up my radio before.

She won't hear me. Maybe she can see me? She has video coverage of most of her interior... she's got to have it for the airlocks. That's a safety issue.

And sure enough, yes, she must, because the outer door slides closed. I wish for a whooshing sound—something that would tell me the small room I'm inside of is filling with atmosphere, but of course, I can't hear anything through this spacesuit. My body is a horrid patchwork of numbness and pain, and the goddamned warning bleeps are still assaulting my ears, warning me that I'm perfectly capable of asphyxiating inside this spacesuit, even inside an air-filled room on *The Kanga*.

I'm just not sure that I can get myself out of it... not with tingling fingers and limbs that feel more like big rocks attached to me through some sort of arcane magic than an actual part of myself.

But my kids must know I'm here now. *The Kanga* let me in. She'll have told them I'm here... or at least, that something is here...

Unless.

I don't want to think about "unless."

The word "unless" holds multitudes of horrible things that could have happened while I was off visiting the Ll'th'th queen. All kinds of ways my kids could have become incapacitated or... worse.

Dammit. If no one is coming for me, then I need to come for them. I have no idea how long I've been lying here—it feels like an unending eternity of suffering, so hopefully, that adds up to long enough for *The Kanga* to have filled the airlock up with some decent breathable air.

I start rocking back and forth, wriggling like a damned butterfly trying to break out of the shell of its chrysalis. I want to unfold my arms like wings and let the blood rush back into them, but first I have to get this weirdly-shaped helmet off and I can barely manage the clasp with my rock-like fingers. Eventually, after a lot of fumbling, the helmet pops off, and fresh air rushes in. Goddamn, there's a lot more oxygen outside my helmet than there was inside. Thank you, *Kanga*. Everything brightens, which is actually kind of painful. I think the low oxygen levels were helping dull my ability to feel how much pain I'm in. Oh well, gotta move forward.

Next step: start yelling. *"Dammit, Kanga, why isn't anyone in here helping me? What the hell is going on?"*

The Kanga's voice fills the air around me: "Cristobel and Gaby are having an armed standoff. You need to fix it."

I blink.

No rest then.

Also, what? The hell?

Well, at least, this means they're alive, but it kinda sounds like both of my older kids have gone crazy. What could they possibly disagree about so strongly?

I pass the question along to *The Kanga*, "Why? Why are they having an armed stand-off?"

Compared to any organic lifeform, *The Kanga* thinks really quickly, so when she takes a long pause before answering a question, I know it's because she's doing it for the effect.

"Based on my understanding of your personality and the psychological powers in effect here, I think it would be better if you approached the situation directly, without a computer trying to explain it to you."

"*What?*" I stop rocking back and forth on the floor. This conversation suddenly requires my whole attention. "You're not just a computer," I say.

"Regardless," *The Kanga* answers.

"Well, that's ominous."

"Very," she agrees.

"And that's worse."

"You should get out of the airlock and see to our family before something irreversible happens."

"You're sending incredibly mixed messages," I grumble as I get back to trying to wriggle my way out of the Ll'th'th-shaped spacesuit. "Aha!" I exclaim, as I get an elbow free. "First, you're just a computer, and then you're part of the family... I'd say make up your mind—" My whole left arm pulls free! "—but I'm afraid you'd choose wrong. Because there is a right answer here: *you are part of my family.*"

The Kanga has had a bad history with organic lifeforms mistreating her. I can't entirely blame her for still being shy and dodgy about whole-heartedly believing how thoroughly she's a part of this family. But damn... her insecurities are being a bitch to me right now. And seemingly, she has nothing more to say.

So, I keep struggling and wrestling with this poorly-fitted

spacesuit until I manage to extricate myself. Shaky and numb, I lurch into a standing position and stomp on the discarded spacesuit, lying strewn on the airlock floor in an ignominious heap, for good measure. That'll teach it.

I'm still wobbly, but if Jaimy and Cristobel are pointing guns at each other—and what else could "armed standoff" mean?—then there's no time to waste on frivolous things like being able to feel the feet I'm walking on. Nope, I'm gonna just throw one foot forward after another, dropping them like anchors, and hoping they hold me upright. I stumble out of the airlock, and immediately hear Cristobel shouting:

"*Not without Janice!*" The sound of her voice echoes down the main hall, coming from the common area at the end.

"I'm here!" I call out. "Whatever you don't want to do without me, I'm here, so, uh..." I trail off, because I don't actually know if I should recommend doing it, since I have absolutely no clue know what we're talking about. But Cristy is alive and shouting, and that's better than things in here could have been.

"Janice?" There's a warble in Cristy's voice. Like she's ready to break. It's a sound that breaks my heart, before I even know what's causing her so much pain. I keep stumbling down the hall, leaning against the wall when I can. Blood is rushing back into my feet, and that makes them hurt, but also, I think my balance is getting better.

I lurch into the common area and find exactly what The Kanga described in her two carefully chosen words, "armed stand-off": Cristy's holding a pulse rifle aimed at Jaimy, and Jaimy's aiming a sonic gun right back at her. Cristy's placed her feline body—smaller than mine—in front of the s'rellick kids' eggshells, where all the children, including the visiting caterpillar, two lizard boys, and Max are all huddling together. Jaimy's larger canine bulk is positioned closer to me, standing near the entrance to the common area. Kth, our adult Ll'th'th visitor, has placed herself off to the side, almost but not quite between my two armed children, just out of the line of fire. Her candy-colored wings are spread wide, instead of falling behind her like a cape. There are green eye-shaped patterns on the inside of her wings, making her look like a giant creature staring us all down.

Spreading wings in response to a threat must be an instinctive Ll'th'th behavior. In all my years on Fathomscape, I've never seen it before. Brief flappings, yes, but holding them wide like this? No.

"So, uh, what's going on here?" I ask with a leading tone. Neither my canine nor feline child looks at me; their eyes are locked on each other. "*The Kanga* told me I had to ask you. So, I'm asking."

Jaimy's the first to speak, "*The Kanga* is afraid she'll have to vent all of us into space, because Cristy is being a goddamned sentimental *fool*." She spits the final word, like it's the worst insult she can possibly imagine. Spoken in that tone, it sounds filthier and crueler than the bluest swear word a pirate has ever uttered. "So, I can see why she wouldn't want to talk to you about it."

Cristy bristles. Her fur's already fluffed out, but her posture shifts. I can tell her retractable claws must be out, scraping against the metal of the pulse rifle in her paws.

"Okay, so, what're the guns for?" I ask, trying to keep an even, calming tone while my own heart is racing. Pointing a gun at one of my kids is enough to make me want to tear someone limb from limb... and right now, both Cristy and Jaimy are doing that. I want to save both of their hides... so I can murder both of them myself.

Max blurts out, "Jaimy wants to kill A'nu!"

"*We have to*," Jaimy woofs, soft and broken. It doesn't sound like she wants to kill A'nu. But it definitely sounds like she believes we need to, and I know what that means. I don't know how it's possible, but I know what it means. My worst nightmare. Scarab infection.

"How?" I utter, though the question doesn't matter. I kneel down and reach toward the cluster of young ones, A'nu especially. "Show me."

My little lizard boy toddles forward; his caterpillar friend, Kalithee, clings with several stubby, fleshy arms to his scaly arm and follows. T'ni stays cowering behind with Max.

Max's hair is short now, I notice. It looks good. Cristy did a good job of cutting it. I want to tell Max so... but this isn't the time. I'll have to remember later.

I feel lightheaded.

A'nu falls into my arms, and I hold his small, cool body close to me. I run my hands over him. All over his body, his arms, his back, everywhere. I can feel the lumps through his clothes, and I can see one on by his collar bone. "How?" I ask again. "Did—" I can't say the rest of the words, but they're supposed to be, "—break aboard and infect him?"

Finally Cristy speaks, her voice is lower than usual, hollow and broken: "The Kanga thinks it's a latent infection—something that happened while he was still in his egg, back in the hatching caves on that horrid moon."

"How did we miss it?" My hands keep moving over A'nu's small, precious body, like if I can find all the tumors, somehow I could collect them up and make them go away. Leave him perfect. Leave him safe. And healthy. "How did we miss *these*?"

How *fast* have they grown? Should I have noticed them this morning? Last night? A week ago? If he's been carrying this infection since he was in his egg, shouldn't one of *The Kanga's* routine health scans have caught it?

But she wasn't looking for it.

We didn't know a baby could carry this infection for this long, starting from before hatching.

A'nu could have carried this infection for a hundred years, since long before I was born. He's always been doomed.

A child doomed to die, and we didn't know. We hatched him, held him, coddled him, taught him, and loved him.

And his death was always living inside him, growing, preparing to break out and possibly take us all down with him.

Jaimy's right. He has to die. He's going to die anyway. The least we can do is find a way to make it kind. Not like this with guns and fighting and conflict.

A bedtime story. A lullaby. Something soft and caring. Loving.

I hate everything I'm thinking. Everything that's happening. And somehow, my hating it, doesn't make any of this stop. It doesn't make the tumors go away.

"Are we sure?" I ask. "Could it be something else?" Anything else.

"We did an x-ray," Cristy says. "They're scarabs."

"The Ll'th'th call them Dor'ecki," I say, uselessly, just saying words to say words, to deflect from the reality of the child in arms who can't last much longer.

S'rellick live long, long lives. Unlike my canine and feline children, A'nu should have outlived me. And Max. T'ni and A'nu should have been together, still brothers, flying through the universe aboard *The Kanga*, long after all the rest of our family is gone.

So many years lost.

So much loss.

And Jaimy's right—so's *The Kanga*—the clock is ticking. If these tumors burst out of A'nu's skin, we're all in trouble. Subtly, I let my wandering, clinging hands press against one of the tumors, checking its firmness, pushing at it, trying to tell just how ripe it is. How long do we have? Long enough for a gentle goodbye? Or... I shudder. I don't want any of this. Enough people were already dying today; we didn't need another one. One who matters more to me.

I think about all the sweet, adorable, funny things A'nu has done—wearing a broken piece of his eggshell like a hat for weeks; tugging T'ni's tail when his brother looks away. He's a jokester. A funny little kid. And so, so sweet. The way he can curl right up against me when he falls asleep...

I don't want him to die. I don't want to kill him.

He'll die anyway...

"We can't kill him," Cristy says, as quiet as she can, but she can't say it to me without saying it to the room, the whole room, including the child shaking in my arms.

I don't know how much A'nu understands, but he's clearly scared. He should be. But also? He shouldn't be. He's a child. Even if his condition is fatal, even if he has to die, he doesn't have to die scared.

"You have a cure up your sleeve?" I ask Cristy, voice high and manic, breaking on the final word. I know she doesn't. I tried to remove these things from Tyler—Jaimy's previous companion—back on Hell Moon. If it can be done, it's beyond us. Beyond the tools we have, the skill, the time...

"Remember Gaby," Cristy says, and her words are like a gut punch because *of course* I remember Gaby. I remember Gaby all the time. I can't make it through hardly a single hour of a single day without missing Gaby as sharply as a knife. But Cristy continues, "What happened to her... and with the s'rellick... their... *ghosts*..."

Horror starts to fill me as I understand what Cristy's trying in her roundabout way to get at.

There were s'rellick ghosts wandering the caverns beneath the surface of Hell Moon who'd been there for a hundred years. Lost and slowly fading.

"...they last so much longer," Cristy says. "We can't do that, not to A'nu."

And now I get the standoff, because she's right? If we kill A'nu—no matter how gently, how kindly—right now, the spectral energy of the growing scarabs under his skin will fuse with him, instead of emerging in the form of baby scarabs. He'll rise as a ghost. A poor, sad baby ghost who will never grow older and won't understand what's happened to him. We know from Ahn'ssi's ghost trying to follow us out of Hell Moon's star system that he won't be able to travel fast enough to ever leave this system. He'd be tied here, by a destroyed space station. And how could we leave him? Our baby, T'ni's brother...

But how could we stay? With Fathomscape on the verge of destruction, this star system won't remain habitable, not really. We need to go somewhere else, somewhere with more people, with a functional civilization. We can't huddle here beside a trapped baby ghost for the rest of our lives.

But how could we leave him?

And the alternative... oh god, it's worse. If my baby has to die, he deserves a gentle death... not scarabs bursting forth from under his skin, tearing his body apart, shredding him with agony and pain.

I've seen a man die this way. I don't want to see it happen to a child.

"Could we... sedate him?" I ask, squeezing my arms tighter around his body. His caterpillar friend has accepted that she's not part of this embrace, but she still hovers by my knee, placing small, grabby hands on me, as if impatiently reminding me that she's there and would like to play with her friend again.

"I don't know," Cristy says. "We'd have to be careful." She's saying that if we gave him too much of a sedative, he could die.

We can't fully and completely take away the impending pain without also risking his life. And if he loses his life too early... before the pain commences... he'll trade minutes of physical torture for a century of mental anguish.

Ahn'ssi was miserable. She didn't want to be ghost.

Maybe...

It's a horrible thought, but maybe, maybe A'nu's too little to care? Maybe being a ghost isn't so bad if you're too young to really understand the alternative?

I shake the thought away. It's a lie. And even if it's not, the rest of us would be tortured by having to leave his tiny ghost behind, floating alone in an empty star system.

"Okay, lower your guns, both of you," I say, because nothing is getting fixed like this.

Cristy lowers her gun. She's a good cat who's been with me since she was just a teen.

Jaimy, though, doesn't lower hers.

"Come on, Jaimy," I say. "I'm not gonna give you a clean shot here, and you know it. This needs to get figured out, and guns don't help."

"I'd have shot Cristobel," Jaimy says. "I'll shoot you too. This needs to be done, *and you know it.*"

I can hear echoes in her voice, shades of recrimination. She knows I watched Tyler die and failed to do anything to stop it. She thinks she's being kind here, saving A'nu from that fate, and she knows she's being wise. Protecting herself, *The Kanga,* the rest of us. I won't be able to argue her out of holding that gun. And yeah, I believe her that she'll shoot right through me to get to A'nu.

You can't fight that kind of conviction. All you can do is humor it.

And oh god, it aches knowing how much it must be killing Jaimy to tell all of her family that she'd happily shoot them. I mean, obviously not *happily,* but still. She already feels like she isn't fully one of us, because she only joined Cristy's and my family a year ago, even though I keep telling her the little ones and *Kanga* have only been a part of our family for that long as well.

There's just pain everywhere right now, isn't there? All around me in every crevice of our lives.

Except for Max's nice haircut. That's one little meaningless tiny piece of joy. I look over at Max, and he's sitting cross-legged on the floor between the two leathery eggshells. T'ni is curled up in his lap, their limbs all tangled together, clinging to each other in this terrifying situation. Smooth skin and rainbowy scales.

I look down at A'nu and see the purple galaxies of his eyes stare at me unblinking, uncertain, questioning. I need to find answers for him and everyone else here.

There's only one answer. It's horrible, but it's the only one we've got: I need to inject A'nu with a sedative, put him in his spacesuit... and eject him from this ship. As long as he's aboard when he dies, the scarabs will escape and begin eating The Kanga's innards like they did before. We can't lose our spaceship. Lose your spaceship in deep space, and you die.

It's A'nu's life or all of ours. Jaimy's right. But Cristy's right too. I tell her, "Go get a get a sedative and A'nu's spacesuit."

A strangled sound escapes Cristy's throat, but she doesn't argue. She lays the pulse rifle down, trusting my body around A'nu to protect him from Jaimy's sonic gun, and she heads to the med bay.

"What's happening?" Max asks. He's the only one other than the three babes in the room who doesn't get it.

I don't want to explain. It's too cruel. Too cold.

Too necessary.

But also, I know, I'll never forgive myself for what we're about to do.

At the same time, I can feel it already—the transition to the other side of this unthinkable action. Deep inside I'm already distancing myself from A'nu, telling myself a new story about the future that doesn't have him in it. A version where he's just a memory, a story we tell to T'ni when he's older about the brother he had a for a short while, a brother he barely remembers.

A'nu is still in my arms, real and breathing, but also, he's started to feel like a shadow. Something I don't want to forget, but also, something I can't stand thinking about.

He's going to be with Gaby soon, lost to me, except in memory.

I'm trying to skip past the pain of A'nu dying, by acting like he's already dead. It won't work. But my brain tries to protect me from what will be a catastrophically painful event anyway.

10

Cristy returns with the small spacesuit draped over one arm and a syringe held in her paw like it's something hideous, disgusting. She's not wrong. She's holding a piece of A'nu's death in her paw, but also, peacefulness. Hopefully, enough peacefulness to protect him from the pain.

Oh god, I can't believe I have to let go of this child in my arms and release him out into deep space to die alone.

Jaimy is growling, low and guttural. I don't know if she knows she's doing it—is it a warning? Her way of complaining that we're moving too slowly? Or maybe she's just upset by what she's seeing, what's happening. We all are. We all have to be.

Cristy kneels down beside me and drops the small spacesuit to the floor. She keeps the syringe in her hand, holding it like it might bite her if she's not careful. It wouldn't be safe to leave something like that rolling around on the floor with its needle and breakable glass barrel filled with sedative.

I take the syringe. Cristy doesn't need this responsibility. This job is mine.

"Hey, A'nu," I say to the child nestled in my arms. He's hidden his pointy face in my armpit. "Hey, little guy, buddy..." Oh god, I sound like a preschool teacher trying to lure a kid out of hiding in the bathroom. A'nu deserves better than this. But this is all I have to give him. "Do you understand what we've been talking about?" He shoves his little snout further under my arm. He's never seemed this small before. He's always been small, of course, but he's also always been bigger than T'ni. In comparison, he was the bold, swaggering, outgoing, braggart of a child, compared to T'ni's timid cowering.

Right now, curled in Max's arms, T'ni looks like the strong, tough one. Yes, he's cuddling with Max, but also, his eyes are bright, clear, watching me. Watching all of this. He's exuding a weird confidence. Good. He's going to need it. I don't want A'nu's death to break him.

It feels like it's going to break me.

And Cristy.

And Jaimy... I glance over at her, and her eyes are glistening. This will break her for sure.

Kth has lowered her wings a little, now that there's only one gun still being waved around. And of course, that gun is pointed right at me. A'nu is the tiny bullseye in the middle of my arms. I just need Jaimy to wait a little longer... give us just a little more time.

"A'nu, can you look at me?" I ask the bundle of shimmery scales curled up in my arms. He shakes his little head, as much as it can be shaken while tucked under my arm. I want to see his eyes. Those purple galaxies. They won't exist much longer; I want to see them one last time, drink them in, try to hold onto the memory of them forever. But I can't force him out from under my arm. I can't fight and struggle with him, not as the last thing we do, the final moments we share.

I feel A'nu's body shift in my arms, and I squeeze him tighter with the hand that isn't holding a syringe. My hand brushes over one of the tumorous lumps, and... did it move? Do we have less time here than I think?

Why today?

Why do I have to deal with this today, while Fathomscape is literally exploding beside us?

"Cristy—" I say, shifting A'nu's weight in my arms, leaning him toward her. She understands my indirect request for help and holds out her arms; she takes A'nu into her furry embrace. With his face removed from its hiding place, A'nu quickly shifts to hide his muzzle under Cristy's arm instead. He won't look at any of us.

Why should he? We're about to send him to his death.

I start singing a broken version of one of the s'rellick babes' favorite lullabies, flubbing all the words and mixing up different pieces of the melody. I can't think straight enough to sing it right, but he deserves to go to sleep for the last time with a comforting sound in his ears, something other than awkward silence and Jaimy's unhappy growling.

I take the syringe, bury its needle between his scales, and shove the plunger in, filling his small body with chemical sleep. He tenses for a moment, but only a moment, and this his whole body relaxes. It happens so fast. I wish I could have talked to him longer... told him a story that would somehow make this make sense, make it okay.

But nothing could make this make sense. Nothing could make it okay.

At least, he's not worrying now. Without consciousness to animate him, A'nu's small head lolls out from where he hid it under Cristy's arm. His eyes are open. They're always open. Such strange little people, these lizard babes with their lidless eyes. I can see the purple galaxies now—they're dulled in a different way than by simple, natural sleep. He's drugged. I drugged him.

I drugged my baby, and now, I need to shove his limp, trusting little body into a spacesuit.

I can't do this. I have to do this.

Is his brother ever going to forgive me? Am I?

"T'ni, Max, do you want to come say goodbye to A'nu?" My voice is shaking as I saw the words. Cristy's whole body is shaking. Gently, I take A'nu from her arms, passing the empty syringe back to her. With A'nu cradled limply in my arms, I grab hold of the little spacesuit.

Without A'nu anchoring her to the room, Cristy rushes off. That last embrace was her goodbye, and it's over now. I envy her. I'm a little mad at her too. I could use her help here.

Max and T'ni have gotten very quiet. They understand about guns. I own enough of them that any kid who lives with me has to be taught early. Taught safety. Taught to stay away from them. And Jaimy still has a gun pointed at me, so Max and T'ni are being good. Staying back.

"Jaimy, you need to lower that gun. You need to let Max and T'ni come over here to say goodbye."

"He's already asleep," Jaimy says. "He can't say goodbye." She doesn't lower the gun. She's a headstrong dog.

"*Jaimy*," I say the word with all the command I can shove into it. It will have to be enough. It is.

Jaimy lowers the gun. Kth folds up her wings and rushes forward to grab Kalithee; the caterpillar child is still huddled at my knee, where I've been ignoring her. It must've been hell for Kth watching her child waltz right into the middle of that standoff. If it had been me and my child, I'd have done more than stand there with my wings spread—no matter how impressive those wings were. But then, I'm loaded up with weapons and have the training to use them. For all I know, Kth is a maintenance worker who's never seen a sonic gun or pulse rifle in real life before. And hell, I don't know what kind movies she watches; if they're all romcoms, maybe she's never seen one in a video before either.

It's not fair to judge another mother for handling a high stress parenting situation involving multiple guns differently than I would have.

But I do. She should have rushed over and grabbed her baby, swept Kalithee away from the area of highest danger. It was her duty as a parent to put herself between danger and her child. Instead, she froze.

I won't let myself freeze. I want to take A'nu into room, lay him down on my bed, and curl around him, protect him from the universe with my body. But my body is no protection from the death growing inside him, and if I wait out his sedative until he wakes up again—oh how much I long for him to wake up again—then I'll just be putting us all in danger.

Besides, Jaimy wouldn't let me. She'd pick up that gun again and shoot right through me to euthanize him. She holds me accountable. Even though she's spent the last twenty minutes—five minutes? an hour? who knows—pointing a gun at me, she's a good dog, and I know it. She only meant the best for all of us, even A'nu.

Finally, tentatively, Max leads T'ni over. Then something shifts when they get close enough to see in A'nu's eyes, and both children throw themselves around him, pulling and hugging as if they might yank him away from me. But I keep ahold of him. After moments that feel like decades, I ask Jaimy to lead them away. She shepherds them over to Kth and Kalithee.

"This is horrifying," Kth says in her singsong voice, three crying children huddled around her. "Are you really—"

"Yes," I say, quickly, not wanting to hear her ask out loud if I'm really going to dump my baby out an airlock to die alone in empty space. Given what I last saw of Fathomscape Station, he'll be far from the only person dying today. I bark a harsh, derisive laugh, aimed at the cruelty of the universe. It's a terrible time to laugh. It's a terrible time to do anything.

I stand up, A'nu still in my arms and his empty spacesuit hanging from one hand. I walk down the hall, back toward the airlock, a funeral procession of one. I don't know if it'll be hard to dress A'nu in his spacesuit. It'd be easier to just— No, no, I can't just blast him into space without it. He'd die. And then he'd become a ghost. I have to keep him alive for the worse, lonelier, more painful death that awaits him.

And yet... no one is following me. No one else wants to help with this horrible task. I glance over my shoulder and, sure enough, Jaimy is standing at the end of the hall watching me, still holding the sonic gun, though not aiming it. She's making sure I follow through.

But she wouldn't care if I didn't dress A'nu in his spacesuit, as long as I got him off the ship. She wouldn't tell anyone. It would be our secret. And if there were a sad, tiny ghost lost in the infinite stretches of deep space, haunting the exterior of the remains of Fathomscape Station... would it matter?

I think of Gaby, those last moments before her ghost disappeared, freeing her.

It would matter to me.

I get to the airlock, and it opens without me doing anything. *The Kanga* is watching, has been watching all of this, and she approves of my plan. She doesn't want A'nu's tumors to be released inside her.

I step inside the airlock, kneel down on the metal floor, and feel the pressure behind my eyes that signifies tears are coming. I can't let them come just yet, blurring my vision. I need my eyes to see the little clasps on A'nu's spacesuit. I need my fingers to be nimble enough to work them. I can't fall apart just yet.

I spread A'nu's pliable cold-blooded body out on the airlock floor. I rest his head on the crumpled up Ll'th'th spacesuit that brought me home like it's a pillow.

You wouldn't expect a cold-blooded child to be as cuddly as A'nu. At least, I hadn't expected it. I guess, because the s'rellick babes are cold-blooded, maybe they're more likely to seek out heat sources like a bigger body to cuddle near. Regardless, I'm going to miss feeling him curled up against me.

I gasp—a sort of hiccough—unable to keep the waves of pain away, and tears spring to the corners of my eyes. I can't keep them back anymore, and my vision blurs. Furiously, I try to wipe the tears away—try to hold them back. I can't feel this yet, but also, I can't stop myself.

Then everything gets worse—A'nu stirs, restless, uncomfortable, in spite of the heavy sedation. For him to feel anything through the sedative I gave him, it must be a massive amount of pain. I may not have much time. I take hold of his little arm and start pulling the baby-sized spacesuit onto him, but he fights back. Squirming and wrestling and making it impossible to shove his arm into the sleeve. Then his body bucks, back arching, and a scream unlike anything I've heard from him before tears out of his throat, rending the world with his expression of pain.

I've heard A'nu cry from discomfort, displeasure, or just general unhappiness before. I've never heard him make a sound like this. And I know: it's too late. My hands start shaking too badly to do anything useful. I couldn't force him into the spacesuit now even if his body went limp again, instead of stiff as rigor mortis from pain and tension.

His eyes like tiny purple galaxies stare at me, and I think he's too drugged to really see—also maybe in too much pain to process anything outside of his own body—but all I see in those eyes is recrimination, like he's asking, "*How could you do this to me? How could you let this happen? You're my parent, you're my god, it's your job to stop me from ever feeling this much pain.*"

I've failed A'nu. I've failed us all.

The lump by A'nu's collar bone starts to bubble, his rainbowy scales melting, and without a coherent thought, I reach out and press my palm against the boiling tumor, as if I can stop the baby scarab inside from bursting out. Instead, the acid melting through my baby's skin burns my palm. I yelp and jump back, palm still burning.

A'nu's wail of pain falters, his body bucks, and the scream stops as abruptly as it started. He's gone. My baby is gone.

"No!" I scream, throwing myself toward him, thoughtless of anything that makes sense. I can't shove his life back into his body now that the spark has gone out, and I was in this airlock to shepherd him towards his inevitable death anyway. Regardless, I throw myself over him, as if this death were something simple like a Saturnian buffalo-ram charging toward him, something I could block with my arms and solid back.

For a moment—a horrible, wonderful, terrible, confusing moment—I think I feel his small body still breathing under me. He still smells the same, faintly of a sea salt, just a little different than his brother. It wouldn't be a kindness for him to still be alive—not to him. But for me, frantic and heart-aching like I've lost Gaby all over again, I grasp at any thread back to his life I can find. Then I realize: the movement I feel under me isn't A'nu stirring; it's the scarabs still forcing their way out through his infinitely precious skin.

I think I'm still screaming, so I can't start screaming again. Then I feel my clothes pull tight around me; the neck of my shirt chokes off my scream by strangling my throat. The world whirls, floor falling away and walls swinging past me, until I'm out of the airlock where I get dropped unceremoniously back on the floor. Jaimy yanked me out, like a kitten grabbed by the scruff of its neck. She slams a giant paw against the airlock controls, and the door slides shut. I hear the sound of the airlock blasting without having cycled out its air.

A'nu's in space now. Buried among the stars.

"Did any of them get out?" I ask. Even with A'nu's body still warm—as warm as a cold-blooded body ever gets—I know what the priority is now. We need to make sure I haven't killed us all by murdering *The Kanga* with my delaying.

And what did the delay buy us anyway? A'nu still died in pain. He was terrified before I drugged him to sleep, and he woke up to insurmountable pain.

He'd have been just as well off if I'd shoved him unceremoniously out the airlock as fast as possible, with no regard for his fear and confusion and impending pain.

But it might have saved the rest of us.

If only I'd gotten back from visiting the queen faster... Could I have operated that stupid spacesuit more effectively? Could I have stayed more focused on my goal and gotten inside *The Kanga* without first passing out? Would that have bought us enough time to do this better?

Maybe, maybe if I hadn't let myself be dragged away by those guards to visit the Ll'th'th queen at all, then maybe we could have made it through this disaster without quite so much screaming.

"I don't know if any of the scarabs escaped," Jaimy answers brusquely, clearly mad that we're in a situation where we have to wonder. She blames me. She must.

I blame me, and I don't know how I could have done this better. There wasn't enough time, and also, even with all the time in the universe, I don't think I could ever have handled shoving A'nu out an airlock to die painfully and alone in the coldness of space well.

Is it better that he died with me in the room with him? Did that matter to him? Could he tell?

I know he couldn't, but I decide, maybe, to pretend that he could. That he knew I was there and I loved him. Still love him. Always will.

"Where's Cristy?" I ask. "The... the kids?" I stumble over that second question, because the word 'kids' doesn't mean the same thing anymore. It means Max and T'ni. No A'nu. The fundamental nature of language has changed, because my baby is gone.

"Cristy locked herself in her and Max's room," Jaimy says. "Kth is watching the little ones."

"They heard..."

"The screaming, yes. Everyone heard." Jaimy's voice is gruff and rumbly—she's still mad at me—but there's a softness underneath too. Sympathy. Shared pain. She lost her little brother today. We all did.

"We have to check..." I start to say, but trail off too tired. I'm still sore and achey all over from the ordeal of stuffing myself into that Ll'th'th spacesuit. I thought that would be the hard part of today. I was so naive.

"...for traces of the scarabs?" Jaimy finishes for me.

"Yeah, like holes in the airlock they might have burrowed through to get into *The Kanga's* innards." I can't really believe that any of them escaped, because if I believe that, there's no where safe left within reach. We'll all die.

When Reeth's scarabs infested *The Kanga* back on Hell Moon, we were able to wait for *The Kanga* on the surface while she went up into the sky to blast her innards with vacuum. That's when I lost Gaby. While waiting for *The Kanga* to come back down for us. But now? All that's in reach is a crumbling space station.

I picture those deadly scarab tumors. They'll have A'nu's baby face on them, sketched onto their coin-sized wings like a cameo carved into mother of pearl, twisted and screaming, like he was right before he died. I don't ever want to see those wings.

I know I need to stand up, look through the windowed door of the airlock, and try to determine if there are any tiny scarabs in there. I know that if they are in there... checking sooner means more time to try to put together a survival plan rather than just, I dunno, waiting for The Kanga to lose patience with us and blast us all into space right alongside A'nu.

I don't want to float out there with the tiny scarabs who killed him for all eternity. That's not the way I want to die.

I'm exhausted, but I pull myself off the floor, leaning against the wall all the way up to standing on my feet. Jaimy's already staring through the window. Her flopped ears are perked forward, her jowls tight—a look of serious concentration. Gaby used to get a similar look, and seeing it on Jaimy's face confuses my heart. My heart's too tired to know what it feels.

I look through the window too. The airlock looks the same as ever, just open to the blackness of space. I shiver realizing A'nu's floating out there—I don't want to see him like that. I've already spent enough time looking at his corpse today. I guess I'm lucky that the air that blasted him out, blasted him far enough way to make him disappear in the darkness out there. The darkness between stars.

"I don't see anything," I say. But am I really looking? I was looking for A'nu, not traces of scarab vandalization.

Jaimy lifts a paw and points. She doesn't say anything. At first, I'm confused; then I realize, she's pointing at a rupture in the metal just inside the outer doors, which are still open. It's small, the size of a coin, but big enough for a scarab to have burrowed through.

Jaimy isn't talking, because she knows *The Kanga* is listening. She's afraid a single word might be enough to send us hurtling through the airlock with the rest of the air, objects that aren't glued down, and people aboard The Kanga following fast behind us.

I don't think *The Kanga* would do that though. I think she wants to keep us alive. I believe she's part of this family. I suspect she's mourning A'nu right now, just like we are.

Well, maybe not just like us. She thinks faster; maybe she feels faster too. I don't know. But she watched that baby hatch and grow over the last nine months just like the rest of us. She loves us, and whatever passes for a heart in her algorithms has to be aching nearly as much as mine.

Suddenly, I don't have energy anymore, and I let myself fall against Jaimy. I wrap my arms around her giant, steady bulk and I cry into the thick fur of her neck. I feel her shoulders shaking, quaking against me. She's crying too. She's shaped like Gaby was, and her fur—now that she keeps it short, instead of shaggy and filled with mats hiding grenades—feels like Gaby's... but she's nothing like Gaby.

Gaby would have found a compromise with Cristy, would have worked things out before I ever got back inside. She was a peacemaker—a big softy. Maybe too soft sometimes. I think that maybe her compromise would have been to just let Cristy have her way, and maybe we'd be even worse off than we are now.

Jaimy's more hardened, tougher, and more able to make tough choices. I should have listened to her earlier, more than I did.

"I'm sorry," I say. "You were right." No matter what we did— we couldn't save A'nu. But we could have saved the rest of us.

Jaimy says nothing, just nods and wraps her arms around me too. She squeezes me so hard, my rib cage aches.

I let us have our moment. But a moment is all there's time for. So, I pull myself together—for Cristy's sake. For T'ni and Max.

Whispering into Jaimy's glossy black fur, I say, "If we can see it in there, so can *The Kanga*. If she wanted to blast us into space, she'd have done it by now. She's waiting. Hoping she won't have to. Hoping we'll figure out a way to fix it."

"There isn't time for waiting," Jaimy whispers back, her voice a rumble I can feel when I'm pressed up against her this close. I needed a hug, and Jaimy gives good ones. I think she needed one too.

"No, you're right, there's not," I say. "But I think *The Kanga* spends a lot of time waiting for us. Waiting for us to catch up with her. She may be so used to waiting that she doesn't know how soon she can risk prodding us to pull ourselves back together." As I speak, my voice rises to a volume I know *The Kanga* will hear. I pull away from Jaimy and raise my gaze, looking for one of the pinhole cameras I know are placed all around the ship. I want to look The Kanga in her eyes—what passes for her eyes—and make sure she understands I'm grateful.

"Thank you for waiting," I say. "Now, we need a plan."

The Kanga's voice emanates from somewhere near the ceiling: "At least three of the scarabs have survived and worked their way into my machinery. I can't track them. We know from experience you can't catch them. I must—"

"Blast them into space, yes, I know," I say, finishing her sentence. I could never have cut her off if she hadn't slowed down to let me. She didn't want to be the one to say it. I can sympathize with that.

"I cannot return to Fathomscape Station and dock." *The Kanga* doesn't equivocate or explain. Jaimy and I both understand the implications, and if she's telling us it's not safe for her to dock—that it's simply not something she can do—there's no point in arguing with her. She knows. And her safety right now is the same as our own. We can't risk *The Kanga* without risking ourselves.

So, we need a way to survive her blasting the scarabs already eating their way through her innards with vacuum.

For a moment, my brain skips a beat, like it just can't believe any of this is happening, like I've just woken up and can't remember where or when I am, because I know—I *know* deep down inside—that I can't be here. It can't be now. This can't be happening.

And yet, it is.

"We don't have spacesuits for Kth and Kalithee," Jaimy rumbles. She thinks she's saying that we'll have to let them die. God, she's a tough dog. Fortunately, she doesn't have to be quite that tough—we don't have to be that cold-hearted, cutthroat, and brutal in surviving the ordeal today has turned into.

"Actually, we do have spacesuits for both of them." I point to the airlock window, indicating the space beyond, where A'nu is resting now. His spacesuit—unnecessary for him now—should be floating near him, and also, the horrible Ll'th'th spacesuit I came here in. "We just have to fetch them. Kalithee can wear..." I can't say A'nu's name right now, so I just don't. "...and well, I escaped the inner ring of Fathomscape in a Ll'th'th spacesuit. It should be perfect for Kth."

Jaimy snorts, probably picturing me wearing a spacesuit shaped to fit a moth. To be fair, the sight was probably pretty funny. Too bad nobody got to see it. Too bad everyone was too busy dealing with A'nu's death throes to come appreciate me lying on the airlock floor, stiff and numb, crammed into that ridiculous spacesuit.

I can imagine a much better version of today. So many different, branching versions of today... all of them better.

This particular version of today that I'm being forced to live through has to be one of the worst possible versions. And I just don't get a say in that. It's like the universe woke up this morning and was like, "How can I make sure Janice has a really bad day? Oh, and also everyone on Fathomscape Station. Let's ruin ALL of their days!"

"Spacesuits won't be enough," *The Kanga* says. Her voice doesn't have a lot of tonal inflection, so maybe I'm imagining it, but she sounds just about as haunted by today as I am.

"Yeah, I know," I say. "We need replacement air."

"That's right," *The Kanga* agrees.

You can't exactly store an entire replacement atmosphere aboard a spaceship. If *The Kanga* blasts all her air into space to kill the scarabs inside her with vacuum, then she'll just be without an atmosphere until she can find a way to replace it.

Sure, our spacesuits will have a little air in them—several hours' worth—but that's not enough to get us to another star system that has actual habitable planets where *The Kanga* could restock.

"We're going to have to go back to Fathomscape—in our spacesuits, I'm not asking you to dock—and steal ourselves a replacement atmosphere." I didn't think I'd ever set foot on Fathomscape again, but I don't see any other way here.

"It won't be safe," Jaimy says, making me wonder what exactly she, Cristy, and *The Kanga* saw while I was gone that made them decide the situation had gotten bad enough they needed to disembark and abandon me.

Gods, they must have thought they'd never see me again. No wonder Cristy is such a wreck right now. And assuming we all survive this, Max is going to have whole new layers of trauma painted onto his personality. T'ni... well... honestly, he might be young enough to mostly not remember. Though, the fact that he hatched from an "ancient egg" as the s'rellick call it does mean that there are some weird, unexpected quirks to him. Those extra hundred years baking inside his egg mean he hatched different, and I dunno, maybe he'll have super-memory and remember all of this.

God, I hope not.

"Do we..." I can't ask it. I have to ask it. "Do we know T'ni doesn't have a latent infection from his egg too?" Each word feels like ash in my mouth as I say it. I barely get all the words out.

"We ran comparative scans in the med bay as soon as Cristy noticed the tumors," Jaimy says. It looks like her words taste like ash to her too. "T'ni is fine. Should be fine."

I look closely at Jaimy's face. I think she really believes T'ni isn't infected. Given how careful Jaimy is that should probably be good enough for me. But the question is just too important, so it's not. And I ask, "Kanga, do you agree with that assessment?"

"Yes," *The Kanga* says. "Scanning A'nu showed me what I should have been looking for. I am confident to a high degree that T'ni is not infected."

"A high degree?" I ask.

"A high enough degree that I do not mind him continuing to live aboard me," *The Kanga* clarifies. And to be fair, that does seem like a pretty high degree.

"Okay, good," I say with relief. I'm gonna try really hard to not lose any more babies today. One was already too much, and even though we're still in the middle of a horrendous catastrophe I'm setting a clear goal: no more deaths in my family. Not today.

"I'll go get the spacesuits," Jaimy says, finally pulling away from me. Part of me wants to protect her from going out there where she might see A'nu... but more of me can't stand the idea of doing the job myself. So, I rationalize that one of us needs to go pass the plan along to everyone else, and I'm better suited both to dealing with Kth—an outsider in our group—and to coaxing Cristy out of her locked room

"Thank you," I say. "I'll go deal with the others..."

"Good luck." The way Jaimy says it, I can't tell if she's being sincere or sarcastic.

I can't tell if she's about to fall apart or if she's a safe rock to lean on. I can't tell much of anything right now. It's like all of my internal sensors have been blown out by all the over-the-top emotion of today. More emotion than my brain and body can process or properly feel. It leaves me walking through the day like I'm on autopilot. I hope that will be good enough...

Given the first half of this day, I don't think it will be, but also, it's all I've got.

11

I head down *The Kanga's* central hallway, steeling myself to pound on Cristy's locked door and shout at her until she comes out—alternating threats with pleading, if I have to. But the door to her room is wide open when I get there, and no one's inside.

I head further down the hall to the common area at the end, but it's empty too. So, I try the bedroom we keep the baby s'rel-licks... I mean... well... Okay, I can't think about how T'ni's room isn't a shared room anymore. I'll just think of his room as "the nursery." I check there, but again, no one. *The Kanga* is a small ship, so unless somehow everyone's decided to camp out in my room or Jaimy's room, they have to be on the bridge.

That's where I find them.

Max and Kth are working computer stations, very focused, with lots of text and images streaming past them on various screens. Cristy's sitting cross-legged on the floor with both T'ni and Kalithee climbing on her feline self. I'm still mad about the way she stormed off earlier, but the sight of her comforting the babies diffuses some of the steam from my boiling anger.

To be fair, my anger is probably more volatile because...

well... damn, how does every single thing I think seem to lead back to A'nu, floating alone and dead in the coldness of space? A cold so thorough it makes his little cold-blooded body seem toasty warm in comparison. At least, the memory of it. The reality...

Dammit, dammit, dammit.

I think about the name of a room, and I'm picturing A'nu floating dead. I think about how I want to snap Cristy's head off for walking out when I needed her, and I'm picturing A'nu.

This is bad, and I need it to get better fast. I don't have time for grief, not until *The Kanga* is decontaminated and filled with a fresh, replacement atmosphere.

No more dead babies today. That's the goal. So, I take a deep breath, re-center myself, and try to box up all the thoughts of A'nu in a storage compartment so deep in my soul that they can't get to me. Not right now. Later, when there's time to fall apart.

"Cristy," I say, "you're out of your room." It's a passive-aggressive way to start. Swiping at her now is totally unnecessary and not helpful... but somehow, that was the best opener I could manage.

"I'm sorry," Cristy says. "I..." She shakes her head, triangular ears flattening. "I thought, well, I realized that we should start downloading everything we don't want lost from the Fathomscape computer networks. So, I wanted to get to work on that, but Max is really better with computers than I am, and then Kth—"

"Your Kanga ship and I are with the collaboration," Kth sang. The melodic quality of her voice that used to seem so pretty makes me want to punch her in her curled-up straw-like proboscis mouth now. Nothing deserves to be pretty right now. Not with...

I block out the image of A'nu. Put it in the box, deep in my soul. Postcards of thoughts to sort through later, when the emotions are less immediate.

"What are you collaborating on?" I ask, and then the full meaning of Cristy's sentences hits me: "Wait—communications are back up?"

"Yeah," Cristy says, tickling Kalithee in her long, squishy abdomen while T'ni climbs onto her feline back and clings on like a backpack. "I guess the traffic has... uh..." She's trying not to say, 'died down.' I can tell. "...slowed down enough that we can actually get through."

For a beat, I know we're both thinking about how the slowed traffic is because enough of the people who were frantically trying to contact each other over the computers have died.

Cristy's voice gets small, quiet. "Your messages came through. All of them. I wish..." Her ears would flatten, but they haven't un-flattened from before. "I wish we'd seen them as you sent them."

"Yeah," I agree, also quiet and soft. Maybe it wouldn't have really changed anything... maybe we'd still be in this situation, because honestly, I would have sided with Cristy and dragged out sending A'nu into space until the last possible minute. And the last possible minute is right next to the first minute when it's simply too late. Too thin a dividing line. Too easy to mess up and find yourself on a spaceship contaminated with metal-eating scarab monsters, because you couldn't accept that a baby you spent the last nine months learning to love always had an expiration date written on his ancient egg, even before it hatched.

The pain threatens to crack me open, so I fake a smile and say, "Have you downloaded the video series about the heartsick robot?" We finished watching it as a family recently, and I think we'll probably want to watch through it again.

"Of course," Max says, not even looking up from the computer she's working at. "Also, the one about the s'rellick spies and the one with the colony that discovers a sentient fungus, and also, everything that looks like it'll be educational for T'ni, and now I'm trying to download a poetry archive for Jaimy..." Her words—ugh, I haven't messed up Max's new name and pronouns in hours, but I guess I'm not entirely over getting them wrong—*his* words trail off as he continues busily downloading as much of Fathomscape's stored culture as possible to *The Kanga's* hard drives before the lights on the station go out entirely.

On that subject, I say, "We need maps. Of the station."

"Already done," Max says, clipped and uninterested in such a boring thing to download. He cares much more about videos and poetry. I hope *The Kanga* has enough storage for all this. I wish we could save it all...

I wish... I mean, while I'm wishing, I might as well wish: I wish we could save all the people too. I wish the station weren't going down in vacuum-suppressed flames.

"*The Kanga* told us about the plan already," Cristy says.

I guess news travels fast.

"I am with the knowing of cargo storage systems," Kth sings. "Thus the collaborating on specific fine points of planning."

"Kth worked in the cargo holds for a while," Cristy says. "So, she and *The Kanga* are working out the best plan of attack for locating and bringing back enough compressed atmosphere to get The Kanga habitable again. Jaimy's fetching some spacesuits? Somehow? I didn't understand that part."

"I escaped the station in a Ll'th'th spacesuit," I say, which is enough to stop everyone in the room cold (except the two toddlers, who aren't paying attention to boring adult words).

"How in the hell did you fit into a spacesuit designed to fit one of *them*?" Max asks, having totally stopped working the computer and instead switched to pointing rather rudely at Kth.

"Very uncomfortably," I say, and then, feeling like some

kind of fool, I add, "Don't swear." Because kids swearing is *definitely* a sane thing to worry about in the life-or-death situation we've found ourselves in. I'd roll my eyes at myself, but it would look like I was rolling my eyes at the rest of them, and no one needs that. "But I left it in the airlock, and it got... uh..."

"Right," Cristy says, connecting the dots. "Jaimy's fetching it from outer space. And also..."

"The other toddler suit," I provide, so she doesn't have to say it.

"Right," Cristy agrees.

Neither one of us could have gotten through those sentences alone. A'nu's brief existence in our lives—nine months of bright sparkling light and joy—is too much of a conversational minefield. Everything here connects to him in some way, because he pervaded our lives. How could he not?

And yet Max is grinning at the computer screen in front of him like the race he's running against time to download as much content as possible, to archive and preserve it for us, is a game and not the library of Alexandria burning. As if his brother didn't just die.

And T'ni is crawling all over Cristy, playing with Kalithee, as if he didn't just lose his only hatch-mate.

Kids are resilient. They're also short sighted. Today is going to be burned into their brains, and it will hurt them later, when they really understand the consequences. Right now, it's as if A'nu were in another room, not gone forever. They can't understand the idea of forever yet. You have to have lived longer in order to extrapolate out to that kind of unfathomable time span.

"That just brings us to the butterfly in the room," I say, turning to Kth. This won't have been the first time she's heard her species referred to as butterflies by a human. As I understand it, they consider it a form of endearment. "I'm not sure you have a home to go back to. I wasn't meaning to invite you to join my family forever... just a playdate. But..." I shrug. It's not like I can kick her and her baby off my ship. Well, not any more than is necessary for decontaminating it.

"The queen still sings hopefully in my mind," Kth says. "But I am understanding your need for replacement atmosphere, and I am having knowledge of where such likeness can be found in disused cargo bay."

I draw a deep sigh. Great. Kth is working a computer station that most certainly can tell her about how dire the situation is aboard Fathomscape Station, and she just watched my whole family almost tear itself to pieces over one of our own being infected by what's infecting the station... But because her queen is delusional and sings into her head, she's delusional.

Cristy, Jaimy, The Kanga, and I are the only sane ones here, and we've all been threatening to murder each other over how dire everything has gotten and our different interpretations of how to handle it. But sure, the queen who brought those monsters here is optimistic.

The bitterness curdles inside of me, and I want to blame all of it on the Ll'th'th queen. But a small, sane part of my brain knows that A'nu's infection isn't her fault. We brought that back with us.

On the other hand, we wouldn't be forced to forge into an exploding war zone for replacement atmosphere if the Ll'th'th queen weren't a damned fool.

A'nu might have been cursed from before he hatched, but everything else that's gone wrong today is her fault and her fault alone.

"Fine," I say. "Your queen is hopeful. What does that mean? You want to guide us to the canisters of compressed atmosphere and then part ways? Does that mean—" I glance at Kalithee all adorably tangled up with T'ni. Even if Kalithee's maggot-like body gives me the creeps, I can still see that the way the two toddlers are playing together—joyfully lost in a moment, blissfully unaware of everything else—is profoundly adorable. It's the kind of moment that makes living in this horrible universe almost seem worthwhile. "Do you want to bring Kalithee with us when we go back to the station on this raiding expedition? T'ni and Max are staying here with Cristy." It only makes sense to leave Cristy; Jaimy's stronger, and someone has to stay with the little ones. I'm not dragging them onto the minefield Fathomscape Station has become. They're safer floating in empty space.

(*Like A'nu...*) I box that useless, painful thought up right away.

Max starts to object to the idea of being left behind, because he's a ridiculously brave kid. But Cristy catches his eye, shakes her head, and he stops. Max might be too shortsighted to see the grief over A'nu that's barreling toward him like a whole plain full of stampeding buffalo-rams, but he can read a room. Damn, he's a good kid. How did I get so lucky to have him fall into my life?

And so unlucky to have A'nu and Gaby fall out?

How can I be both at once?

Life makes so little sense.

"Yes," Kth says in a measured way. "Yes, I should bring Kalithee with me, so when we be staying, we are together. It is our home hive."

Part of me is relieved. I haven't just added a pair of strangers into my family for an indefinite period of time until I can find a habitable planet or non-exploding space station to dump them on—something that might take long enough for them to end up feeling like this is their home first. Hell, *The Kanga* might even get attached and realize she likes this singing moth better than me. Can't have that.

On the other hand...

A bigger part of me knows that I understand the danger

we're facing in a much deeper, more visceral way than Kth does. I can't let her drag her baby back there. Dammit.

"No," I say, setting out to convince Kth of something I don't want to convince her of. "No, it just doesn't make sense. All the kids—" It kills me that A'nu isn't one of *the kids* in that sentence. "—should stay here until we see the situation back there first hand. It's safer. Really. Please, let Cristy watch Kalithee for you while you help us. We can figure out what's best for the two of you afterward."

I can't read Kth's face with its curled proboscis, wriggling mouth parts, and big, spherical eyes like a disco ball cut in half and jammed onto a sculpture from the mind of ancient Earth's Kafka. So, I just wait. Eventually, she shrugs with all four of her arms—a gesture I do understand, because it's one the Ll'th'th on Fathomscape Station picked up from us humans.

"As you say," Kth agrees peaceably. I expected more of a fight. I know I don't want to be separated from my kids during a situation like this—that was already a hard thing I had to struggle with today. I don't exactly want to repeat it. But Kth doesn't argue. I guess Kalithee is staying here.

And that's when Jaimy shows up, dressed in a spacesuit with the helmet down, holding two more spacesuits in her arms—one large Ll'th'th-shaped one and another smaller, toddler-sized one. It's not shaped right for Kalithee, but it'll hold her. She'll squeeze into it about a thousand times easier than I squeezed into the Ll'th'th one. If she were shaped the same as her mom, we might have a problem. But she's got that weird caterpillar life-stage going on, and from the way she keeps squirming under Cristy's arms and tumbling around with T'ni, I can see she'll be squishy enough to fit into a s'rel-lick-shaped suit. She's a lot squishier than me.

Jaimy's eyes look haunted to me, but then, I guess she's looked a little haunted ever since Tyler died back on Hell

Moon. I honestly can't tell if she looks more haunted than usual right now.

"It's time to go," Jaimy says.

"Yes, please," *The Kanga* agrees. "Everyone needs to put their spacesuits on."

If *The Kanga* is speaking up, she must be really feeling worried about the tiny scarabs infesting her innards. *Tiny scarabs with A'nu's twisted face etched into their wings...*

No. That line of thinking stops now.

I reach out a hand toward the spacesuits in Jaimy's paws and take the toddler suit. A'nu's suit. "I'll help get Kalithee dressed, unless you want to do it yourself, Kth. Cristy, can you help T'ni?"

"I can!" Max cries, already having abandoned his computer post to start running through the bridge toward *The Kanga's* central hall and the closet where the rest of our suits are waiting for us.

I crouch down beside Cristy, who still has Kalithee and T'ni crawling all over her and say to the little ones, "We're going to play a game. We're going to put our spacesuits on, and we're going keep them on for a while. Maybe a long while. Okay?"

T'ni's little reptilian face stares at me. He nods. "Spacesuit game," he confirms in his clipped toddler speech, forked tongue darting from his narrow spade-shaped muzzle.

Kth joins our little group on the bridge floor. Her long, spindly limbs bend sharply as she crouches low enough that her abdomen lays along the floor. Her sharply folded limbs make her look especially angular. "You will be staying with nice cat, yes? Good cat, good child, you be good too," she sings to her caterpillar. Kalithee toddles into her mother's four spindly arms. It's an awkward embrace—at least, it looks awkward to me. Maybe the hug is an affectation, picked up from spending so much time around mammalian species. At some level, their whole mother-daughter relationship is an affectation, since most Ll'th'th caterpillars are kept in the inner ring, being raised by an entirely different biological class of their species.

Even so, their goodbye embrace is touching.

When it ends, I hand the toddler suit to Kth, but since she's unfamiliar with its design, I also help undo the various fasteners. Kalithee's limbs are too numerous and short to fit a s'rellick-shaped suit well, but her body squished up in the torso of the suit pretty well, extruding out into the wide base of the part of the suit meant to hold a long tail. And toddler suits are made with a fair amount of flexibility—parts that can be either cinched up tight or loosened—so the suit can grow with its owner. I help cinch up the arms as tight as they go, so Kalithee will have a chance of operating the gloves. And we loosen the tail up as much as possible, since Kalithee's caterpillar body fits better into the tail than the legs.

While Kth and I are doing this, Max has already helped T'ni into a suit and half dressed himself in his own. Cristy disappears and comes back in her own suit. As does Jaimy. By the time Kth starts pulling on the "borrowed" Ll'th'th suit I took from the inner ring, Max is already back at his computer station trying to keep downloading more files onto *The Kanga's* hard drives, in spite of clunky suit gloves making his hands clumsy. I bet he's going to keep trying to do that even after The Kanga blasts out her atmosphere, even while Jaimy, Kth, and I are gone fetching a replacement atmosphere. He's a single-minded child at times, completely focused on the things that interest him, most of which live inside a computer screen, except for his younger brothers.

Younger brother, I correct myself. One. Singular. A'nu is gone. Hate and pain curdle and swirl inside me, mixing up into a toxic potion that threatens to boil acidly in my stomach and lash its way into my throat, trying to claw its way out of me. I try to push the feelings away, push the acid back into my stomach, divorce myself from time and space and reality... and just turn around, make my feet move, and walk myself to the closet by the airlock holding my own spacesuit. It's the only one left hanging there now. We should probably buy an extra, just to have around. It seemed less important a few hours ago, when *The Kanga* was a docked ship that had no reason to leave her comfortable little berth on Fathomscape.

It's too late to buy an extra one now. There's no where left to buy it. Maybe... maybe there'll be somewhere we can loot one along the way to whatever compressed atmosphere stores Kth plans to lead us to.

I put my spacesuit on, and as soon as the helmet is fully fastened, *The Kanga's* voice comes over the suit's radio: "According to my sensors, everyone is fully suited and protected against vacuum. Barring any objections, I will begin a count-down to decompression now..."

I want to object, because hell, my spaceship—my home, my bubble that protects me from the deadness of space—just told me that she's going to vent my only stable source of oxygen. But that's an emotional reaction, not a logical one. I also want to object, because I want to have eyes on all my children and double-check that they're all ready myself. But The Kanga is probably better at checking spacesuit conditions than I am anyway. So, I don't say anything, and *The Kanga* begins counting down from fifty. I don't know why fifty, but I instantly hate the number, just for getting itself involved in such a sordid situation.

I get back to the bridge around the number thirty, and my heart almost stops at the sight I see: everyone's dressed in their spacesuits—one big dog, a cat who stands about shoulder high to me, a similar sized human, a full-sized Ll'th'th complete with those giant wings in their weirdly inflexible covering, and *two little s'rellicks*.

Except it's not two s'rellicks. It's two s'rellick-shaped space-suits with their spade-shaped helmets and long tapering tails, except in one of them, the inhabitant is shaped nothing like the suit. Kalithee's stubby feet are all squished up into the suit's tail, which is why she's sitting on the floor, legs empty and splayed in front of her. And her maggoty face with all its squirming mouth parts is only barely visible in the back of the overly long narrow helmet like some sort of pale-faced nightmare lurking in the shadows.

Seeing Kalithee's face framed by a window that's supposed to look in on A'nu's sweet little reptilian self just makes her creep me out more. But I can't hate her. She's a child, and none of this is her fault. Seeing her just makes me sad, so sad, infinitely sad. I didn't know you could fit this much sadness inside a person. I sure as hell wish you couldn't. I wish it would overflow and drain away. Instead, somehow, the sadness keeps finding more places inside me to well up and congeal. Someday, I won't be a person anymore; I'll just be a person-shaped avatar of walking sadness.

The Kanga's countdown reaches zero, and nothing seems to change. Inside our spacesuits, this deep into the ship, with nothing around that isn't attached directly to The Kanga's skeleton, there isn't much change to see. It's not like I can feel the air rushing past my bare skin. My skin isn't bare.

Of course, we'll have a mess to clean up in the other rooms later. Everything stirred up by the sudden draining away of the air. Oh well, that's a problem for later, after we've all survived.

Because we are all going to survive. No more dead babies. Not today. And goodness help me, never again.

"Have you got this under control, Cristy?" I ask over the suit radio.

"Yes, I've got this," she says. I wonder if her ears are still flattened inside her suit helmet. After the day we've been through, it seems likely, but all I can see are the suit's ears. Triangular, standing tall. They make her look happier than her voice suggests she is.

"Okay," I say. "We'll be back soon."

Part of me wants to make a big deal out of saying goodbye to Max and T'ni, dragging this whole process out and savoring every little bit of them I can soak up of their personalities and physical presence, despite two layers of spacesuit getting in the way.

But most of me knows that making a big deal out of a goodbye in a situation like this is just asking for crying kids who get all stressed out and worried about us not coming back. It's better to assume we'll come back, and so no one needs any precious tearful goodbyes.

So, after a moment of trying to memorize them with my eyes, I turn away from my family—most of my family—and head towards the already-open airlock with Jaimy and Kth right behind me.

12

Before we reach the airlock, Jaimy and I stop at another closet in The Kanga's main corridor—one we keep thoroughly locked, since small children live onboard. We don't even have to talk about it; we just both know: we need to load up with weapons. We're heading into a collapsing space station, filled with people who haven't died yet... but are gonna. And they know it. And they have nothing left to lose.

I sling a flamethrower over my back, strap a sonic rifle to my left leg, and holster a pulse gun at my right hip. Jaimy chooses her own assortment of weapons. I know the flamethrower is probably overkill, but it'll look impressive if there's a big crowd I want to deter from following us or want to clear out in front of us. Usually, it wouldn't be safe to use any of these weapons aboard a space station, but the station's already going down. We're not gonna make it a whole lot worse, no matter how much damage we do.

I gesture welcomingly at the closet of weapons and say over my suit radio, using a closed loop so it's only audible to Jaimy and Kth, "You're welcome to outfit yourself too."

Kth says, "I think I'll trust in you two to protect us."

"Suit yourself," Jaimy says, gruffly. For a second, the anger in her tone makes me think she's blaming Kth for the queen's actions, bringing the scarabs here. Which is rich, given that it was Jaimy's artwork that led the queen to knowing about the scarabs in the first place. Anger flares in me at Jaimy's careless-ness, posting those pieces of art where anyone could see them and learn from them.

Then I remember that no one else here knows about what the queen has done. Or do they? I can't remember what I said in all the messages I sent before I left the inner ring... Even though that was only a few hours ago, it feels like a lifetime. I guess, in a way, it was. A'nu's lifetime.

I shake thoughts of A'nu out of my head. I'm getting better at brushing those thoughts away like unwanted mosquitos, biting and stinging and causing me pain that I don't have time to deal with.

It's not that I don't want to think of A'nu. I want to think about him for hours, just dwelling and remembering and savoring. But... I don't want to think about the end of his life. I want to think about who he was, and the good things he brought into our little world—the way he made the universe better for the short time he existed.

Except... I realize, I'm staring off into space, and my chest is tightening. This isn't helping. I don't have time for honoring A'nu's memory anymore than I have time for being haunted by it.

Regardless, my thoughts of A'nu have driven my anger at Jaimy away, and that's probably for the best. I don't have time to remonstrate with her about cyber security right now anyway. My mind is a mess, and I wish I could just turn it off.

I add one more weapon to my artillery—a laser cutter, so more of a tool than a weapon really—also strapped onto my back, and then we're ready. We don't have to open the airlock; it's already open wide.

It's so wrong for both doors of the airlock to just sit open like that, like *The Kanga* is a derelict vessel, stripped down by salvagers and left to rot in the darkness of space.

Oh gods, I hope no one comes by and tries to salvage her while Jaimy and I are gone. Cristy is trained with weapons—I made sure of that—but she's not the protector that either Jaimy or I would be. It's times like this that I wish The Kanga were equipped with more weaponry on her. Still, she could probably play chase, outrunning and hiding from anyone who tries to board her, other than us. As long as she sees them in time...

She didn't see me. Not until I pounded on her airlock door controls.

I open a radio channel to Cristy and say, "You should keep an eye on the external sensors while we're gone. Just to be safe. You know, make sure that nobody but us approaches you."

Cristy says back, "I'll have Max do it. He'll love it."

"Already on it," Max says.

The Kanga adds in her fluid yet artificial voice, "I'm sorry I didn't notice you outside earlier. I've already made adjustments to my algorithms to make sure I won't make the same mistake again." After a moment, she adds, *"Come back safe."*

The Kanga doesn't usually add niceties like that to what she says. I know she has feelings, but she doesn't usually express them. In this case, I guess she's saying: "I don't want to watch the children slowly asphyxiate aboard me, because you didn't bring back oxygen for them to breathe." And honestly, that's a totally fair thing to get emotional about, even if you are a big metal spaceship.

Clearly impatient with my dithering, Jaimy leads the way, launching herself out of the doubly-open airlock like she's diving into a swimming pool. I climb out of the airlock after her, and kick off of The Kanga's hull. I assume Kth follows behind, but I don't look back. I can't tear my eyes away from the crumpled, scorched, wreck of a space station in front of me—

both because it's the kind of train wreck you just can't look away from, and also because I know A'nu's out here, and if I let my gaze wander at all, I'll be looking for him. I won't want to be looking for him, but I will and it'll hurt if I see him... and it'll hurt if I don't. So, best to stare at flickering fires I can see through the windowed parts of Fathomscape's rings that haven't been blown out by explosions.

Yes, that's right, there are clearly fires raging aboard the intact parts of the space station. Why? I don't know. Maybe explosions caused by the metal-munching scarabs munching the wrong things, maybe someone's misguided attempt to fight back against the scarabs, or maybe just the result of infighting between angry people who know their time is counting down.

We're heading into that inferno. It's growing larger with each passing second, as I sail away from my hollowed-out, airless home.

Suddenly, I realize that I forgot to tell Max his haircut looks good. I'd meant to tell him before leaving, but... somehow there wasn't the time, or maybe my brain just can't hold onto something that small and frivolous right now. But it's not really small and frivolous. It'll mean a lot to Max, and I should have said it. But somehow, radioing back as we're sailing away to say something like, "Hey, Max, your haircut looks good," feels too much like an admission that I don't know if we'll make it back. It feels like it would jinx the whole trip. Besides, I want to see the grin on Max's face when I tell him.

But maybe... holding onto to those words like they're too frivolous to cloud up such a serious goodbye is the real way to jinx ourselves.

I've always believed you should never put yourself in a situation where your death would be ironic. The universe fleeking *loves* irony. Fortunately, irony only exists when there's a mismatch between your expectations or knowledge and the wider context of knowledge available, so if you always expect—

or at least acknowledge the possibility of—things going horribly wrong, then it won't be ironic when they do.

Basically, the universe loves smacking us when we're down, especially if we don't see it coming. So if you always expect the universe to step on your neck with its big heavy boots, then at the very least, you rob of it of the satisfaction it would get from surprising you.

Maybe that's a small comfort, but I cling to it sometimes. If the universe wants to snap my neck, it's not gonna see a look of surprise on my face as its happening.

And yet, I never saw A'nu's death coming. With all the fear I'd been harboring, living with every day, the idea that A'nu had been infected by the scarabs before he'd hatched, before I'd even rescued his eggs, never ever occurred to me.

You can't protect yourself from the dangers of irony. They're everywhere, coming from every direction.

Kth sails past me suddenly, filling out that oddly-shaped spacesuit perfectly, adjusting her course carefully with small blasts of its jets. She zooms ahead of Jaimy too, taking the lead. Then her voice, as lilting and lyrical as a flute solo, comes over the radio, "Follow me. I am toward the disused airlock, close to our destination, flying. Follow, follow along."

And so we do, adjusting course with our own suit jets, wibbling and wobbling on a jagged course through the empty space between *The Kanga* and the outer ring of Fathomscape Station. Kth is leading us toward one of the parts of the station that looks most whole, most untouched by the chaos ravaging the rest of the three rings. The middle ring—where I've lived all my life—is in the worst shape. I don't know how the Ll'th'th have managed it, but even though they're the source of the destruction, they've kept their ring—the inner ring—in much better condition. The lights are still out, but at least, fire isn't flickering behind them and there are none of the cavernous cavities pockmarking the inner ring that have ravaged the middle one. The tell-tale traces of the explosions I watched happen earlier.

The closer we get, the less of the station I can see. The portion of the outer ring we're flying toward fills my vision, blocking the view of the more damaged parts of the triple rings. I'm grateful for that. Finally, Kth zeroes in on a specific airlock —it's large enough for a ship to dock at it, not designed for individual entrance and exit like the one I escaped the inner ring from. But that makes sense—we're looking for the kind of big cargo that would get loaded and unloaded from long haul carrier cargo ships. It's gonna be trick moving it around with just Kth, Jaimy, and me, but hopefully we can find some antigrav dollies to help. That's the kind of thing you'd find in a disused portion of a cargo bay full of forgotten canisters of compressed atmosphere, right?

Well, if not, we probably won't have to worry about gravity for too long. It looks like the rings are slowing down their spinning. Theoretically, once you get a space station like Fathomscape rotating properly, it should keep doing it for a long time —momentum plus lack of air drag resistance adds up to just spinning and spinning forever. But I think the various explosions have acted like jets, messing with the station's proper spin. Of course, I guess that could mean heavier gravity... or just erratic gravity... I'm glad we didn't bring the kids with us. They're better off on *The Kanga*, even if she doesn't have any air for them to breathe. This mission is going to be dangerous.

Kth slams into the side of the station first, but Jaimy and I follow right after her. Immediately, she starts trying to work the airlock door controls, but I can see it's not going well. I don't know if her codes are out of date, because it sounded like she hadn't worked in this part of the station for a while or if the mechanisms have broken down due to the damage growing and spreading across the station.

"How old are your codes?" I ask.

"Only a several of the months," Kth sings. "I worked here before, when I Kalithee found. Is how I found her sweetness, near here."

I can feel my brow crinkle. None of that sounds right. "What?" I ask. "What do you mean? *Found* her?"

The Ll'th'th keep their children on the inner ring, tended to by an entire biological class of their hive. I don't see how Kth could possibly have found a stray egg or even hatched caterpillar all the way out on the outer ring in a cargo zone. Toddlers may be troublesome and prone to wandering, but not wandering *that* far.

But Kth doesn't answer me, because before she can, Jaimy unholsters her own laser-cutter and starts cutting right into the station's hull. She's never gonna cut all the way through the full width of Fathomscape's outer shell with that little tool, but she will be able to get us better access to the control panels for the door, hopefully making it easier for us to hot wire ourselves in. I could keep pursuing the confusing question of how Kth *found* Kalithee way out in this part of the station, or I can help.

I want my own kids to live through today, so I help.

Jaimy and I burn into the metal beside the airlock door, methodically moving our lasers toward each other until the line of melted metal meets. Jaimy turns her laser cutter around, juts the butt of the tool against the panel, and it cracks, skewing enough that I can get a gloved hand around one edge and start yanking the piece we've cut all the way out.

Jaimy, of course, reels away from the station, thrown backward by the answering force to her laser cutter hitting the side of the station. She jets back quickly enough, and the three of us make short work of pawing through the circuitry we've revealed under Fathomscape's outer skin.

We get the outer airlock door open. All three of us jet inside, where the momentum of the outer ring's continued spinning feels like gravity. Maybe it's lower than it's supposed to be, but I'm not sure. It feels pretty normal, but then the gravity on the outer ring should be heavier than what I'm used to, much in the way that the inner ring's gravity is lighter.

I can't tell if it's heavier.

I can tell that the lights on the other side of this airlock's inner door are dim and flashing red. So, that's not good. It's also not surprising. I'm gonna count it as good luck if we can get in, get out with some replacement air, and manage to not have to actually interact with anyone else along the way.

Maybe that's selfish. Maybe once we get some replacement air, The Kanga could save more than just us. More than just my family plus Kth and Kalithee.

And maybe I don't fleeking care. There are too many people dying to care about them all, and too little time to think through and prioritize how to pick and find a few specific ones who I could stand inviting to join us on our ship.

This day is going to be a scar for more than just the kids. I'm going to be hating myself for being selfish right now, in this very minute, for a very, very long time. I'm going to be wondering—could I have done more? Could I have done better? Could I have saved even one single whole-ass person who is otherwise going to die today?

And the answer right now is no. No, I can't. I have to stay focused. But the answer tomorrow? And the day after that? I have a cold, sneaking, awful feeling that the answer is going to change on me, just as soon as it's too late to do a single goddamned thing about it.

Kth convinces the outer airlock door to close much more easily than we convinced it to open, and then, as if by magic, she gets the inner door to open just as easily. And like that, I'm back aboard the station I'd already written off as gone.

Time to loot a ghost town.

13

I pull my spacesuit helmet off and leave it hanging, dangling behind my head. The helmet is really more like a hardened hood, so that works okay, which is good, because you don't want to get too far away from your helmet in a situation like this.

Kth and Jaimy do the same. I want to remonstrate with them both—really chew Jaimy out for being careless with her art and really drill down and find out what the hell Kth means about *finding* Kalithee. Something about that word—*found*—just really rubs me wrong, and I want to figure out why. But we need air, not to shoot the breeze, so I hold my tongue and keep it from wagging needlessly. We can have those conversations later, when *The Kanga's* full of air again.

Kth leads the way forward, walking at a brisk pace through the abandoned hallways here, taking us from passageway to passageway, passing by one giant hangar of cargo after another. I want to tell her to hurry up, but she's already walking fast, and it's not like running at full speed through darkened corridors with flashing red lights is the safest idea. We don't need any twisted ankles slowing us down because we were in too much of a hurry to be cautious.

Occasionally, I hear the echoes of voices. They sound ominous, threatening. I can't tell if that's something real in their tones, or if it's something I'm projecting. I look over at Jaimy, walking briskly beside me, and I see the alertness in the set of her jaw, the angle of her flopped over ears, and the tightness of her jowls. She's scared. Probably a lot of other feelings are flooding through her too.

Watching her and the profound concern painted in clear letters all over her face, I realize that I'm never going to tell her how the Ll'th'th queen found out about the scarabs on Hell Moon. She doesn't need that kind of responsibility, that heavy of a weight, resting on her shoulders. She carries enough as it is.

She made an honest mistake.

A mistake that small should never have consequences this big. And the lesson she'd learn from the connection between her action—simply sharing a piece of her art with the world—and what all this has come to would be much, much, much too much. She'd never share her art with anyone again. She'd close down. The last flicker of hope and optimism in her bulky canine body would fizzle out, and she'd become a shadow of who she could otherwise be.

Her gentle artists' soul should be nurtured. Not squashed down by this kind of weight.

She's not the one who brought the scarabs here.

The queen did that. The queen should have known better.

Suddenly, screaming like a flute played by overzealous, angry five-year-old, Kth falls to the floor. Jaimy and I drop down on our knees beside her, trying to figure out what's wrong, what happened.

"Are you hurt?" I ask.

"Did you trip?" asks Jaimy.

Kth's moth-like head rocks back and forth, shaking in a gesture that could be communication or might just be spasmodic convulsions. I can't tell which. I can't tell what happened to her, but we don't have time for it. I grab one of her foremost arms and try to help her up, but Kth shakes my hands away, flailing her arms and clawing at her head with her suit-gloved talons.

"The silence!" Kth cries. Her voice still sounds like a flute solo, but it's taken on a haunting keen to it, like something dying. A funeral dirge, played over a coffin being lowered into the ground.

And I realize what must have happened: the queen has stopped singing in her mind.

I flip my helmet back over my head and expand my suit's radio channel to include *The Kanga* and those aboard her and ask, "Can you see anything that's changed aboard the station from where you're at?"

"Yeah," Max says, youthful and callous as a child can be, "it's all falling apart and blowing up and a total mess."

"No," I say, "I mean something that happened *just now*. Just before I called you."

There's a moment of silence and then Cristy's voice says, "Nothing specifically changed in the last few minutes. It's just been a continuous, slow, steady downfall ever since the series of explosions that happened before you came back onboard."

I remember those explosions. I hope nothing like that happens again while we're still here, dealing with whatever is happening to Kth. Returning to my theory that her pain has something to do with the queen's singing in her head, I ask, "Does Kalithee seem okay? Nothing's happened to her?"

Another moment of silence happens that feels far, far too long. Long enough for me to worry that there actually are going to be more dead babies today. Even if Kalithee isn't mine and kind of creeps me out, I sure as hell don't want her to die.

"Kalithee seems fine, Janice," Cristy says. "Everyone here is fine. The little ones and I have been playing a pretend game where we're starwhals flying through an asteroid belt, and Max is still downloading as much content as he can onto *The Kanga's* computers."

"If you happened to bring back some external hard drives to store some of these files—" *The Kanga* interjects "—I certainly wouldn't mind. Though, obviously, replacement atmosphere is the priority."

"I'm gonna fill *The Kanga's* memory so full of vid series that she won't be able to beat me at video games anymore." I can hear the grin in Max's voice as he speaks.

"You can try," *The Kanga* replies, "but if you do, I'll just start deleting files I don't think you really need."

I wish I were back home with my family, bickering about video games. But I'm still here, surrounded by flickering red emergency lights and listening to Kth's horrifying yet beautiful out-of-her-mind screaming.

I'm about to turn off the radio channel and flip my helmet off my head again when Max says, "Oh, wait, I think I found what you must have been looking for: all the message boards just lit up with it. It's all anyone can talk about. Geez, I've never seen so many people all talking about the same thing at once on the Fathomscape socials."

How can that kid say so many words about a topic without actually saying what the topic is? Max infuriates me sometimes. "What, Max? What are they talking about?"

"The Ll'th'th queen has been..." He trails off, and I don't know exactly what he's failing to say. I don't know exactly what's happened, but I know I was right. Something has stopped—or changed—the singing inside Kth's head.

But apparently, it hasn't affected Kalithee.

Kalithee who Kth found somewhere around here, on the outermost ring, as far away from the secretive, secluded Ll'th'th nurseries as you can get and still be aboard Fathomscape Station.

That child is not Ll'th'th. I don't know that for sure. Maybe children don't hear the queen in their heads the same way adults do. But didn't Kth tell me that her queen has been singing in her head since she was a child? Since she was in her egg?

Maybe it's not that then. Maybe there's just something different about Kalithee, like how T'ni and A'nu hatched from ancient eggs, making them different from other s'rellick.

But I know none of that is true. I know that child is not a baby Ll'th'th.

I've seen her kind before, in a ghostly vision, in ancient murals painted on twisting cave walls, deep under the surface of Hell Moon.

I don't know how it's possible, because Kth clearly found Kalithee months ago, and the Ll'th'th queen only brought back her shipment of "Dor'ecki" from Hell Moon a few weeks back.

But Kalithee is a Dor'ecki maggot; the other half of the scarabs' life cycle.

I knew there was something wrong and unholy about the immediate attraction between Kalithee and A'nu. She sensed their connection. That has to be what happened. The maggot child sensed the tumors growing inside my own baby, and she knew they were connected to her. Surrounded by humans, uplifted cats and dogs, various avian aliens, and a pair of s'rellick babes, she honed right in on the poor child who was incubating tumors that shared her DNA and would ultimately kill him.

I want to kill her.

Instead, I pull my suit's helmet back off. I think Max was still talking, rambling about the Fathomscape social networks or downloading videos and games; I don't know, I wasn't listening. Instead, I grab Kth harshly by the head, laying my hands right on the sides of her giant, silvery, multi-faceted eyes. I turn her toward me, in spite of the fact that I know she must have essentially 360 degrees of vision.

She can't help but see me; my face is right in front of hers, and my gloved hands are blocking out her peripheral view. I wonder what those eyes feel like without spacesuit gloves in the ways. I want to squish them. But first, I say, *"What do you mean you found Kalithee?* She's not a Ll'th'th like you. Is she? *Is she?"*

I know she's not, but it's different to hear it.

Kth's screaming chokes off, and she manages to sing a few words, which is good, because if she didn't answer me, I was going to start breaking limbs. I don't think the spacesuit Kth's wearing would have stopped me. "Am meaning what am literally saying—found her, found her near here. Pale, pale egg, like albino Ll'th'th egg. Was alone, all alone, took home to raise myself, be like egg-tender, nursery worker, in spite of assignment to work cargo in outer rings. Be like little queen myself with own daughter. But oh! Now my queen, her highness, her loveliness stops singing! Oh!"

Kth's words broke off, and she began wailing again, like that haunting flute solo, like a creature ready to break into pieces.

"This is no good," Jaimy says. "We need to find the compressed atmosphere tanks whether Kth can lead us to them or not."

As if on cue, in response to the idea that we might leave her behind, Kth stops wailing, rises to her feet, and takes off running. No more brisk pace. Full on running.

Jaimy and I glance at each other, uncertain of what we should do, but not for long. We'd been following Kth. Our default is to follow Kth. So, only a heartbeat later, we're both running too.

Zigging and zagging down corridors, I try to keep Kth's space-suited wings in view, but she keeps getting just far enough ahead that whenever she takes a turn, I lose sight of her for a while before catching up. "Wait for us!" I call out, but it doesn't do any good.

I hear noise coming from ahead—like the sounds of an orchestra tuning before a performance, discordant and beautiful at the same time. Especially if the whole orchestra were composed of woodwinds—flutes, oboes, piccolos, clarinets— all singing together, but also apart, fighting each other with their mismatched tones.

I come around the next corner and screech to a halt at the edge of a wide, empty cargo hold. Empty of cargo, that is. It's filled with Ll'th'th workers, standing in circles, arms raised to the sky—well, the ceiling—and waving in some sort of fervent religious ecstasy. Their disco-ball like eyes glitter, and their candy floss pink and spring green wings flap slowly, stirring in the air and filling my view with complicated, visual noise as neighboring pairs of wings open and close in randomly staggered anti-patterns. I can feel the breezes and eddies caused by the flapping wings play across my face.

Kth has already joined the crowd; she's the only one with her wings covered, but otherwise she fits right in with all these other Ll'th'th, dressed as cargo and maintenance workers, holding their multitudinous, spindly arms high.

"What the hell," I say, a muttered exclamation under my breath. I notice other people around the edges of this Ll'th'th congregation—humans, a few other mammaloid species, a couple s'rellick also dressed as cargo and maintenance workers —all looking as lost and confused as I feel. Were they drawn here by the sound of all the wailing Ll'th'th? Had they been here before this eerie congregation began, still working or looking for ways to survive the end of Fathomscape Station?

I don't know, and I don't want to know. I'm surrounded by dead people walking, and I want to get my cubic assload of compressed atmosphere and get the hell and gone away from here.

I go up to Kth, put a hand on her middle left arm and say, "Hey, we need your guidance here."

Kth doesn't respond, just keeps flapping her suited wings, waving her four arms in the air, and moaning like a flute whose queen flute has died.

"I think we're on our own," Jaimy says, her voice so close that I turn and see she's right beside me. Even so, she's hard to hear over the melodic wailing all around.

"Is it some sort of funeral?" I ask, though I don't know who I'm asking. Kth is non-responsive, and Jaimy won't know.

Though, perhaps I'm underestimating Jaimy, because she's a sharp dog and extremely focused on what we're observing. She says, "I think it's more than that. I think... there are factions?"

As soon as she says it, I see she's right: the Ll'th'th aren't organized into only one group; there are several groups, loosely circling each other, facing off with each other. For a moment, I worry that they're about to begin fighting, tearing each other limb from limb, but instead, the tone of their discordant singing changes, smoothing, coming into harmony. There are still several distinct, different, dominant tones, but it's no longer complete aural chaos. And furthermore, I couldn't possibly miss the way the Ll'th'th have divided themselves into groups now. The groups are tightening, drawing together, still standing in circles, but distinct, separate circles. My anxiety kicks up several notches, and I draw the pulse gun holstered at my waist, dead sure that the groups are going to start fighting.

Then the singing stops. Just stops. No more funerary dirge to fill the air, just an eerie silence.

The Ll'th'th drift away from each other, some of them picking up tools they'd discarded on the floor and returning to some kind of work while others simply leave. Around the edges, a few of the non-Ll'th'th exclaim surprise. I hear several shouts of "What the hell?" echoing my own muttered sentiments from earlier.

Kth turns to me, a sparkle of awareness having returned to her glittering eyes, and says, "It is done. The new queen is chosen."

A shiver travels across my entire body, and I mutter, "Long live the queen, I guess." I can't say I'm sorry the old one is dead. I assume she's dead if the Ll'th'th have chosen a new one.

The new queen must be having a very strange day. She's become queen of her people... and that's probably a good thing? But she's also inherited a mess. She'll be lucky to have a people left by the time the day is out.

Thinking about the day coming to an end makes me realize just how much time has passed already during this disaster, and exactly how long it's been since the last time I ate or slept: forever. That's how long. *Exactly* how long. Unfortunately, there won't be time for rest or food until *The Kanga* is filled with air again. You can't exactly eat inside an atmosphere-free spaceship. You can sleep I guess, but that's just a way of wasting time that we don't have available to waste. Same deal for trying to grab a bite here, where there's still atmosphere—it wouldn't help my kids who are still aboard *The Kanga*, and hell, the atmosphere here could blow away at any second given what Fathomscape looked like from the outside.

"So, uh, now that the queen is chosen..." I say in a leading tone, "...you're ready to lead us to those compressed atmosphere tanks?"

Kth's feathery antennae wave like little conductor's batons. I wonder if its uncomfortable for Ll'th'th to have their antennae curled down, crammed inside a space helmet. It must not be too bad, or they would have designed a way for their antennae to stand up inside the suit and stay protected, like the hardened compartments for their wings.

"I will lead you," Kth agrees. "Your ship must be with the

refilling of atmosphere. You all will need for the breathing."
The way she says it makes me nervous, like she's already
decided she won't be returning to *The Kanga* with us. Maybe we
should have brought Kalithee. Maybe I'm going to get stuck
with a baby maggot as part of my crew. My family.

Child of the enemy, raised beside the child of mine who lost
his brother to her people's heedless, careless, callous, evil
reproduction.

"Don't do it," I say. "Don't leave Kalithee with me."

"She will be loved," Kth says. She turns away and runs
again, before I can begin swearing at her. I run after her, struggling too hard to keep up to have any breath left over to swear. I
had no idea Ll'th'th could run that fast.

As I run, I can't stop thinking: how dare Kth tell me that I'll
love a child who represents the death of two of my own—A'nu
and Gaby. Not to mention Tyler, who Jaimy clearly loved in
spite of all his faults.

No, I don't want Kalithee.

My feet pound the floor as I chase after Kth, and my angry
thoughts echo between my ears.

I don't want Kalithee. I don't want her growing up beside
T'ni, inside *The Kanga*, playing with Max, being comforted by
Cristy, and protected by Jaimy. I don't want her at all. I don't
want her pale pudgy skin, stubby little arms that will grow out
to weird tentacles, or creepy face with its circle of wriggling
mouth parts and black eyes that I had assumed would one day
change to glittering, silvery, multi-faceted orbs like Kth's.
They'll never change. Kalithee will never enter a chrysalis and
emerge as a cheerful, beautiful, candy-colored moth alien.

She is what she is.

A pale, tentacled maggot being. She'll grow larger. She'll
grow into a creature that's supposed to be impregnated by the
scarabs' flickering blue ghostly light, who's supposed to incubate tiny tumorous scarab babies while they grow, who's

supposed to die when they emerge, her consciousness and memories saved and carried on inside the other half of her people's life cycle.

She's the embodiment of my nightmares, and she's back aboard *The Kanga* playing pretend games with Cristy and T'ni.

There's no escape, I think. *The Dor'ecki have already made it to my home.*

And yet, there's a small part of my brain that's still rational enough, still coherent enough to know that's a massive oversimplification.

The scarabs might infect humans, s'rellick, Ll'th'th, and other species when they're starving and crazed, but the maggot portion of their life cycle is completely and utterly harmless. They're gentle creatures, vegetarians even who eat only tubers and fungus. Sweet, soft, and sensitive souls.

The original civilizations the scarabs come from would be horrified by the way their untended children are behaving, eating away the foundations of the worlds they find themselves upon and haphazardly rape-impregnating anything with a vaguely similar heat-print to the maggots who should be tending them, caring for them, treating them like precious loved ones and valued partners rather than the nightmare monsters they've become.

As we run, we pass other looters—I say "other looters" because I know that's what we've become. It's why we're here. Most of them are looting smaller things than what we're looking for. Things that an individual can carry. I know the condensed atmosphere tanks we're looking for will be far too large to manage without anti-gravity, and even then it's going to be a bull to manage.

We get to the end of hallway and Kth stops. She stops so fast, I almost run into her. As I steady myself, she reaches with her four arms so fast—I think she's trying to help steady me—

but instead, she grabs the flamethrower from my back, yanks it off of me, and turns to run again.

I try to shout an objection, but nothing coherent comes out of my mouth, just a primal scream torn from my throat. I don't want Kth—who's been dangerously prone to fits of religious fervor in the last half hour—running around with my flamethrower. Why the hell does she even want it?

When I take off running again, I'm not chasing Kth. I'm chasing my flamethrower.

I don't even need that flamethrower.

And who am I stop Kth from burning the remains of this place to the ground? As long as Jaimy and I can find the compressed atmosphere tanks first, and she doesn't light them on fire...

Stuff like that wouldn't react well to fire.

My feet start to slow, as I give up on the idea that Kth is trying to help us anymore, but they don't come to a complete stop. Some morbid part of me wants to know what Kth stole that flamethrower *for*, and so I keep following her, halfheart-edly, confusedly, just stumbling in pursuit of a crazed fairy-like moth alien. Wielding a flamethrower.

Kth comes to a closed cargo bay door with window panels inset in it; though at this angle, I can't see much through them. She stands in front of the closed door, holding the flamethrower, maybe catching her breath, maybe steeling herself. I don't know.

"What are you doing?" I ask

"Max," Kth says, and I instantly dislike hearing my child's name in her weird fluting voice. I don't trust Kth. I don't trust anyone who steals a weapon right off my back without explaining themself. "Human child explained life cycle. Max knows well?" Kth asks. "Max's knowledge is correct?"

Jaimy has kept pace with me and is standing beside me with two weapons drawn. I still have the one pulse gun in my hand, but I'm aiming it at the floor, not Kth. I don't know why. She stole my flamethrower; she's acting erratically; and she was harboring a Dor'ecki maggot child who she's insinuated into my household and home. I have every reason to point a gun at her.

"Max knows the Dor'ecki life cycle," I say in dull, hollow tones. *"Why?"*

"Then Kalithee will not hurt," Kth says, and I think she's saying that Kalithee won't hurt us... but she might also be saying that we won't hurt Kalithee? There's just too much in this world I don't know. "The compressed air is two bays back. Easy to find."

Kth reaches one of her four talon hands up to the door's controls, and the cargo bay door slides open, revealing a much wider view of the space beyond.

It's filled with eggs. Those pale, translucent, crenelated eggs that look like giant steamed dumplings, arranged in careful, orderly rows. But not just eggs—there are maggots too. Maggots like Kalithee. They toddle among the eggs, chasing each other, playing. I'm looking at a whole goddamned Dor'ecki nursery. The kind of nursery that hasn't existed—outside of the Dor'ecki homeworld, I guess—for more than a hundred years. And in the middle of it?

A monster straight out of my worst dreams—legs and feet as black as obsidian, mandibles as wide and sharp and serrated as saws, and eyes as red as burning embers. The scarab is tending the eggs, turned mostly toward us, but seemingly unaware of the visitors who've entered its domain. The scarab turns a little, and my heart—which was already racing hard enough to beat its way right out of my rib cage—comes to a total and complete stop. I mean, obviously, not literally. I don't die from a heart attack on the spot... but, for a moment, it feels like I have. I feel like I've crossed to the other side of life, a side I didn't know existed, a side beyond reality, because I can't experience this much fear and rage and bewilderment and hold all those feelings inside me. I'm not a big enough vessel to hold that many feelings. They're just too large.

Because, you see, the face etched on the back of the Dor'ecki scarab's metal wings is familiar. I know that face. The reptilian snout twisted into a preternatural grimace of terror on the back of the Dor'ecki's hauntingly beautiful, shimmery metal wings is Reeth's.

14

I've seen scarabs like the one in the middle of this cargo hold before. I've crushed them under my feet when they were no bigger than a coin; small enough to turn into a decorative clasp on a scarf. They burst out of Reeth aboard *The Kanga*, and she abandoned us on the surface of Hell Moon while she flew up out of the atmosphere to blast them with vacuum and kill them all.

One must have survived.

One hitchhiked back to Fathomscape with us.

One of them has been munching on the station, growing bigger, growing strong, reveling in the profusion of metal here for it to eat, and laying eggs that the scarabs back on Hell Moon didn't have enough energy to lay. It's been building this little empire in this cargo hold here for nine months now, far longer than the Ll'th'th queen's shipment of Dor'ecki has been aboard the station.

We doomed Fathomscape. Me and *The Kanga*. By coming here at all. We were the walking dead, and we carried our virus home with us.

The Ll'th'th queen's deadly foolishness has only sped up an end that was already growing in this cargo bay.

Fathomscape Station was already infected.

"Your lowness killed my queen's royal highness!" Kth screams like a flute being blown like a whistle, no musicality, just air tearing through its body and escaping through any hole it can.

Kth fires up the flamethrower, and heat explodes into the room like we've stepped into a furnace. Flames lick over the carefully arranged rows of eggs, burning them, burning the maggots playing between them, searing it all.

But of course, as I could have told Kth, the fire doesn't hurt the fully-grown scarab-form Dor'ecki. I've used flamethrowers on the scarabs before. It might deter them for a moment, but their metal carapaces, black as glass from a volcano, don't burn in fire.

Not like the soft skin of the flailing maggot children which chars in an instant, turning from smooth, pearlescent white to ashy, cracking, red-edged black. Not like the tender translucent eggs which bubble from the inside and burst out like blisters popping, flesh boiled by too much heat. The maggot babies scream. I think I'm screaming too. Screaming for it all to stop, for none of this to have happened in the first place.

Jaimy rips the flamethrower from Kth's talons, kicks the crazed Ll'th'th to the floor, and steps a heavy hind paw on her thorax. I look up and see that though the flames from the flamethrower have stopped, the burning has only begun. The fire is inside their skins now—eggs and maggots both continue burning and burning away. Children the size of T'ni flail and scream and die in front of me.

Children who would never have harmed anyone.

Children who were never asked if they wanted to exist, never given a chance to avoid dying in horribly, flaming pain.

"What have you done?" I ask Kth, the words ashy in my

mouth, but she doesn't answer. No a-grammatical, melodic words answer my accusation. So I look down, tearing my eyes away from the horror in front of us, and see Kth completely crumpled on the floor, no longer restrained by Jaimy's hind paw stepping on her.

Her neck has snapped. Her life is gone.

Did Jaimy do that when I wasn't looking? Did Jaimy press her hind paw down on Kth's narrow neck and end her life?

I can't say the choice was wrong.

We were never bringing her back to *The Kanga* with us after this. And staying here... anywhere on this station... it's a death sentence, almost for sure.

And staying here? Double death sentence, because there's still a full-grown scarab frantically searching through the fire in the cargo bay in front of us, trying to rescue eggs and toddlers... but soon, that frantic energy is going to turn from trying to save what cannot be saved toward avenging what has been lost. And I don't want the scarab to find us on the other side of the fire when it emerges.

"Come on," I say, grabbing Jaimy's arm with my free hand. "Let's go get our air and get the hell out of here."

I've seen hell today. I thought I'd seen hell before, on that desolate moon with three layers of derelict civilizations all underneath a scorching sky. But no. Hell isn't desolate. Hell is screaming. Hell is still alive and both desperate to live and desperate to die, just to escape the pain.

Hell is here.

Hell isn't somewhere far away. Hell is your own home, going down in flames.

Jaimy and I don't run from the fire. We don't talk about it, but I think, we don't want our feet to pound against the floor. We don't want our movement to be sudden; anything that would draw attention in our direction right now is bad.

The last thing we need is a vengeful scarab emerging from

the flames, its metal wings heated by the fire, ready to maul us with its serrated mandibles or infect us with its ghostly, flickering blue light.

The worst terrors can't be run from. You can only walk away, hoping they don't see and follow you, because you'd never make it if you ran.

We get to the cargo bay door that Kth indicated—two bays back the way we'd come. We laser cut our way through since the heavy metal door is locked, and we no longer have someone with us who knows the codes around here.

The tanks of compressed atmosphere are inside, just like Kth told us they would be.

I can't shake the feeling that the scarab will find us any second, and it keeps my hands shaking. My shoulders shaking. Or maybe, I'm shaking because I'm crying? Or exhausted and hungry? My body feels like it could break down, just fall to the floor, and I'd melt into the metal ground, a useless puddle that used to be a human. Used to be a parent. Used to be someone who loved others and was loved back.

I need to finish this task, so I can be all those things again.

Jaimy finds a pair of anti-grav dollies, one for each of us, which is good because the tanks we're stealing are taller than Jaimy and just as wide. Gigantic cubes of compressed atmosphere. Sure, they're filled with the basic atomic stuff that adds up to air... but not when it's compressed to this degree. At this level of compression, it's probably a liquid in there. Or plasma? I don't know that stuff. I'm not a scientist. What I do know is that when I kick one of the cubes, it doesn't budge. When I put my hands against it and shove, it doesn't budge. And when I lean into it with all my weight, feet braced against the ground, I'm more likely to hurt myself trying to move it than ever, ever get it to budge.

Jaimy attaches both of the dollies; one each to a gigantic cube of atmosphere. They click into place attached to the side, thank goodness, as there's no way we're sliding anything under these ridiculously large and heavy boxes.

Jaimy does the work of attaching them, ostensibly because I'm keeping watch, which mostly just means being really jumpy and continually looking over my shoulder, even as I keep turning to check every direction, as if scarabs could come pouring out of any corner or shadow in this cargo hold.

Realistically, though, Jaimy's doing the work, because she's holding herself together better than I am. I don't know if that's because she's tougher than I am, or because she's more damaged so new damage just layers on top of the old scars, not hurting as much, not feeling as fresh. Or maybe, it's just because she's eaten more recently.

Sometimes it's the little things. Hell is easier to survive on a full stomach and a full night of sleep.

Jaimy powers up the anti-grav dollies, and the giant cubes of compressed atmosphere imperceptibly rise off the floor. It's a disconcerting sight, because visually the change is so subtle that it doesn't really register... and yet, suddenly, you can tell something is different, something is wrong. Something that's supposed to be very, very heavy and immovable is suddenly as light as a balloon, light enough to be brushed aside with a feather.

"Let's get out of here," Jaimy says, grabbing the handle on the dolly attached to the side of the giant cubic tank closer to her. "Let's go home."

I grab the handle on the tank I'm standing beside and am about to agree with Jaimy about going home when a train of thought takes me somewhere I really don't want to go.

Home is the only safe place right now—a place with no air and no scarabs, but we can fix the lack of air. The lack of scarabs is what's really important, and we made sure of that by blasting out the air. We blasted out all of Reeth's scarabs with the air. But...

One of Reeth's scarabs is here.

That's when all the pieces click together, in a really unpleasant way, a way they should have clicked together earlier: if one of Reeth's scarabs survived aboard *The Kanga* after she exposed them all to vacuum, then blasting her innards with vacuum isn't enough. "*Holy hell...*" I mutter to myself.

Jaimy looks startled, hearing the dawning horror in my tone, and asks, "What?"

"We can't go home."

"What?"

"It isn't safe."

"It isn't safe *here*," Jaimy insists, clearly halfway convinced I'm having a breakdown and babbling incoherently. "Cristobel, Max, and T'ni are at home. *The Kanga's* the only safe place left."

I shake my head, mouth hardening into a frown. "No, she's not safe. That scarab—" I point with the hand still holding a gun, waving it around in a careless way that I'd usually be better than. "—it came from Reeth. I recognized him on..."

"The wings." Horror is dawning Jaimy's voice now too. She looks like she wants to drop the handle of the dolly and run all the way back to The Kanga without stopping.

But that wouldn't help anything.

"We have to tell her," I say, and we both know—both Jaimy and me—that I'm talking about telling *The Kanga*.

"There's no telling what she'll do if we tell her..."

I shake my head again. "*The Kanga's* family. We have to tell her."

"What if..." Jaimy looks haunted for sure now. There's a glassiness to her eyes, like she's picturing the one way that this day could actually get worse.

We might not have a home to go back to.

We might be stranded in empty space beside an exploding space station.

But what's the alternative?

Withhold this information from *The Kanga* and *hope* that none of the scarabs survive this time?

Hope that if one does survive we get to a habitable planet or welcoming space station before it eats *The Kanga* up from the inside out?

Those are bad plans. And I'm kind of an expert on bad plans. I make a lot of them.

I'm not making this one. I'm calling *The Kanga*.

I flip the helmet on my spacesuit back up, over my head, and open a channel to *The Kanga* and Cristobel. I specifically leave Max and the little ones—T'ni and a child who I haven't accepted belongs to me yet—out of this conversation. Though, I do loop Jaimy in, and since she follows in flipping her helmet back on, I know she'll hear what I have to say.

"I have some bad news." It's a terrible way to open a conversation, but some conversations are so bad, there's no good way in. "We've encountered one of Reeth's scarabs here, all grown up."

"Reeth's scarabs?" Cristobel hisses, fully aware of the implications.

"Yes, Reeth's."

"Are you sure?" *The Kanga* asks, and the sound of her voice drops the floor out of my stomach. This is when she's going to abandon us forever and decide that gliding through the depths of space empty and alone is better than messing about with the complexity of hosting organic organisms.

But I still can't lie to her.

"Yes, I'm sure. It had to have survived when you vented your atmosphere back at Pentathia. I... I don't know what to do. But I had to tell you. You had to know." My words turn weak and watery by the end. Filled with tears I'm not ready to cry yet and nausea that's already churning my stomach.

"What can we do?" Cristobel says. "Do these things just not die?"

"Fly by the sun." Jaimy states her suggestion as such a simple matter of fact, like it's the only option, an obvious option, something we all should have been thinking of even though she was the first to say it.

"If I fly by close enough," *The Kanga* says, "there is a good chance the radiation will sterilize me of any living matter."

"Living matter includes *us*," I object. "It includes Cristy, and Max, and T'ni." And even Kalithee. Though, just because I think her name doesn't mean I'm ready to say it. Part of me thinks she should fry in the sun's radiation as well.

Most of me remembers those maggots flailing and screaming.

I'm better than that. I'm better than Kth turned out to be.

"Yes," *The Kanga* says in an infuriatingly agreeable tone, "the flyby will need to be done before you return with a replacement atmosphere. Have you secured one, by the way?"

I glance over my shoulder at the giant cube disconcertingly floating imperceptibly above the floor. "Uh... yes... but..."

"Excellent," *The Kanga* charges ahead, not waiting for any more of my objections. "Then Cristobel and the young ones will evacuate, and wait for you here. I will return as soon as possible."

I like the sound of the last part of that sentence—the part where *The Kanga* expects to return. I don't like the first part where she suggests dumping all of my kids in outer space with nothing around them but thin spacesuits, waiting for her hopeful but less than certain return.

"I don't like this plan," I say.

"Whether you like the plan or not is irrelevant," *The Kanga* says. An organic lifeform might have snapped the words, impatient and annoyed. *The Kanga* expresses stunningly little emotion as she says, "This is the best plan available at this time, and we don't have time for further discussion. The sooner Cristobel and the others evacuate, the sooner I will return. You don't have enough oxygen in your suits to argue with me until you find a way to feel good about it. It's what's happening. You can sort your feelings out while waiting for my return."

I want to argue with her. I really do. The idea of her ejecting my kids and flying off to dive into the sun is just fraught with so many things I hate that I want to spend hours really tearing it apart.

But that's when the room starts shaking, and then a heartbeat later, gravity stutters. I can't think of a better way to explain it. The sensation of downward flickers, shudders, and outright stops. We're floating. The anti-grav dollies have become totally unnecessary because everything else is floating around us too.

"That had to be a giant explosion," Jaimy says, "to have knocked the spin right out of this ring."

"Oh hell," I say, looking at the readout on my spacesuit's sensor system. "The atmospheric pressure dropped too. The ring's losing atmosphere."

Over the radio, *The Kanga* says, "It was two explosions on opposite sides of Fathomscape's outer ring. The half of the ring you're in is no longer attached to the rest of the station."

Well then. Gravity is not gonna be coming back.

"We have to go. We have to go now." Jaimy grabs ahold of the dolly's handle. Maybe the anti-grav aspect has become redundant, but the dolly also lowers the tanks' inertia. Without it, one of these gigantic cubes would be a bitch to get moving, and once it was moving, it'd be twice a bitch to get it to stop. Without the dolly attached, it would take both me and Jaimy working together to push and shove just one of these massive boxes through the twisty network of corridors we traversed to get here. And that's assuming we could do it at all.

And we need two of them.

Half an atmosphere just isn't enough.

While we've been struggling with our own, new, suddenly pressing problems here aboard Fathomscape, I think *The Kanga* was saying goodbye and Cristy was saying something about herding the little ones outside... And it wouldn't have made sense to stop them, even if I could have, but I'm mad that I missed my chance, because I'm distracted by annoying nonsense like the outer ring of Fathomscape Station losing its structural integrity.

Fine, well, I'll just have to chew *The Kanga* out for her very reasonable plan that nonetheless makes me mad when she gets back. For now, I grab hold of my own dolly and start pulling the giant cube along behind me like it's a puppy I'm taking on a walk.

A walk through hell.

Or really, more of a float, as everything's floating now. Thank goodness for our spacesuit jets. Without them, we'd have a hell of a time getting these cubic tanks moving. We'd have to bounce from ceiling to floor and back, zigging and zagging our way down the hall. With the jets, we can just zoom forward.

I follow Jaimy along one hall after another, carefully maneuvering the box behind me and quietly seething about the idea of *The Kanga* leaving a collection of children floating in space all alone, as if somehow this is all *Kanga's* fault. Sometimes you need a scapegoat, even if you know you're being unfair to them, you just need someone to be mad at for a while. Because being mad at the actual monsters is too scary. It's easier to be mad at someone you love who loves you back. Someone who will forgive you. Instead of, you know, murder-rape-impregnating you.

Through the material of my helmet, I hear screams up ahead—along the path we need to follow—so I check the readout on my suit's sensors again. Air pressure is still dropping, but the atmosphere isn't gone yet. I guess that's why I can hear screams.

It also means spacesuits must be at a premium around here.

"Jaimy, we need to be ready for combat," I say. I'm still holding my pulse gun in one hand, while steering the dolly with the other. Jaimy though re-holstered all of her weapons while attaching the dollies to their loads.

She pulls a sonic gun off her back now. Good, different styles of weapons. It's always good to choose weapons with complementary mechanisms, in case we find ourselves faced with a situation that answers to one and not the other.

Now that we're both armed and ready, we let the dollies' momentum push us forward... Toward the screaming. I wish we could just cut our way straight out of this metal tin can of a station without winding through these stupid corridors, but laser cutting our way through layers of metal would take longer than walking through this maze.

It's just that the maze is filled with monsters—some of whom have been monsters for as long as they've been away from their homeworld, starving to death for lack of enough metal to recreate their original civilization, and some of them just turned into monsters today when they realized their way of life was over and their actual lives would also be over soon, unless they find a way to escape this imploding space station.

Our spacesuits—in spite of already being occupied—might just look like the one way out of this space station to someone who doesn't have a suit of their own and is still fighting not to die.

Monsters are made by their situations. And this is a really, really bad situation.

We get to the end of the hall, and the screaming reaches a fever pitch ahead of us. It's time to fight our way through.

15

We re-enter the chamber where all the nearby Ll'th'th congregated during the picking of the new queen and find an all out, zero gee brawl. There's a human man trying to cut the wings off a Ll'th'th-shaped spacesuit, and while I have some sympathy for the idea, I also know this guy can't be quite in his right mind. Hacking an inconvenient piece of a spacesuit off using a knife isn't going to leave you with anything. Anything at all. A breached spacesuit is trash.

There are also several Ll'th'th and a pair of s'rellick having some sort of stand-off, wielding weapons that look more like construction tools. It looks like they're fighting over ownership of a crate floating between them. I can't tell what's in the crate —spacesuits? Oxygen tanks? Something else? Who knows.

A couple avian aliens spot me and Jaimy with our gigantic crates of atmosphere trundling along beside us, and one of them cocks its birdlike head at an inquisitive angle. Our giant crates of compressed atmosphere are only useful if you have somewhere to fill with atmosphere... but right now? Just barricading yourself up in an isolated room aboard the station with its own source of air might feel like a way to buy yourself a few more days of life, and any extra day of life is an extra day for rescue ships to arrive from another system, looking for survivors.

I hold my gun up high, making sure the bird aliens see it.

They see it.

One of them starts flapping its way toward us anyway. Those feathered arms sure are an advantage in this zero gee free-for-all. Jaimy fires. I'd have fired a warning shot first. Maybe that would have been a waste of time and ammo. Jaimy's harder edged than me. She shoots the bird right in its inquisitive head. My first instinct says: if you have to shoot a civilian, aim for the legs. Legs can be repaired.

But slowly bleeding out while the station crumbles around you would be a pretty miserable way to go. Sometimes Jaimy's harder edge adds up to a weird sort of cold kindness.

Mercy is cruelty; outright assassination is kinder. The world is upside down right now.

Not that 'up' and 'down' even mean anything anymore on this broken fraction of a space station.

The bird alien with a hole in its head topples end over end in the zero gee. Several of the other avians—after stopping and clustering together to check on their friend—also start flapping our way.

It's an unforgivably cold thing to think: but right about now would be a good time for the atmosphere to finish draining away. I don't want to shoot my way through these civilians who are just fighting to survive, but I want to let them get their talons on my spacesuit even less. Even if I win the fight, all they have to do is tear a hole in my suit, and I'm done for too.

Jaimy and I both start shooting, but the sound of our guns draws attention and more people of various species start appearing from behind floating, tumbling crates of cargo and at the other entrances to the chamber. I blast one pulse shot off after another and start to get tunnel vision, imagining that this it—this is the rest of my life, fighting to escape a crumbling, torn-up space station until the whole thing explodes around us, leaving the rest of my family waiting in the cold of space with no atmosphere coming.

Can't have that.

Can't really control whether it happens...

But I can take more control of this situation. "Cover me," I say to Jaimy, while holstering my pulse gun. I pull the flamethrower off my back, and light it up. Sure, the flames it throws are less impressive in the thinning atmosphere, but it still sends a clear message to everyone around: *get back; we're serious.*

Even so, a burly s'rellick manages to work their way around me and tackle me from behind. Jaimy shoots him in the head, just like the avian before. This time, the shot is closer to me than I can handle, and I break out swearing a blue streak at Jaimy over our suit radios.

Like I said, it's easier to blame the ones we love than the people who are actually, actively trying to hurt us.

Jaimy doesn't apologize, but after a beat, I do. There isn't time for more, because that's when Reeth's scarab enters the chamber, metal wings flared wide and saw-like mandibles clacking. The image of Reeth on those wings is split right down the middle, half of his face appearing on each wing. It's a horrifying sight, and I'm profoundly grateful the face on those wings isn't someone either Jaimy or I were closer to—not Gaby, not Tyler.

Though some of Tyler's scarabs *are* on this station. I just hope Jaimy never has to see any of them. They started on the inner ring; we're on the outer ring, so our chances of avoiding them are good.

For now, I flare the flamethrower at Reeth's scarab, but the flames don't deter him like I expect. In fact, I think they're drawing him toward us. Maybe it's still looking for the arsonist who burned down its nursery, and wielding a flamethrower makes me look guilty. I can't say the scarab's wrong. I am wielding the exact same flamethrower that heartlessly murdered its children. The most harmless part of the Dor'ecki lifecycle.

Jaimy starts firing with her sonic gun at the scarab, and I sling the flamethrower over my back again, pulling the pulse gun from where it's holstered on my hip with my other hand in practically the same motion. Both of us firing two different kinds of weapons at the scarab at least slows it down. Without gravity, it's trying to fly, but each blast from a gun—even though the shots don't seem to hurt its heavily-armored, mostly-metal ass—at least propel the giant scarab backward. We're protected from the recoil throwing us around by the anti-inertia aspect of the dollies we're steering.

I'd have us cut and run, but we can't afford to turn our backs on a metal-eating monster with the compressed atmosphere tanks pulled along behind us. If the scarab ate a hole in one of the tanks, we wouldn't have enough atmosphere to fill *The Kanga* back up. When she returns. Because she *will* return.

We need to be there when she returns.

And we need to have all this atmosphere with us.

What we really need right now is a shortcut out of here. We need to blast a hole in the side of this station and forge our own way out.

"Dammit," I say to Jaimy over our radios, "it's times like this I wish you hadn't let me convince you to shave off all your mats. We could really use a grenade right about now."

Jaimy used to have grenades squirreled away all over her body, woven into her dirty, matted fur. Now her fur is clean and short. Such a short-sighted waste...

But then Jaimy rips an extra panel that I hadn't noticed off of her spacesuit—it looks like something she temporarily glued on to its outer surface—and reveals a grenade she'd been hiding, nestled right into the cavity of her armpit.

"Old habits die hard," Jaimy says, pulling the pin out of the top of the grenade. She lobs it in the direction we've been heading, managing to arc it into a perfect curve right down the passage we've been trying to fight our way toward.

Automatically, I count the beats out in my head—by the time I reach five, there's a deafening roar, followed by a sucking whoosh. Whatever atmosphere was left in here is on its way out.

Jaimy's grenade blew a hole right through the side of the station. Moments before, we were stuck inside a death trap, unable to work our way free past the looters, vengeful scarab, and twisty maze-like network of corridors.

Now we're flying into empty space with the rest of the debris, looters tumbling head over tail around us, and cargo crates zipping dangerously by. I hold on tight to my dolly's handle, hoping against hope that I won't lose my grip and lose half our atmosphere. Also hoping none of the debris around me damages the tank.

Also hoping Jaimy doesn't lose hold of her half.

I catch sight of her big canine shape; she's still clinging to the handle of her dolly too. Good dog.

"We need to get clear of this debris field," I say to Jaimy through our open channel.

"I'll follow you," she answers.

So, I fire up my spacesuit's navigation jets and start dodging my way through the cluttered darkness, zipping away from the tumbling corpses as fast as I safely can while lugging a giant tank of compressed atmosphere behind me. I guess, at least A'nu won't be buried out here all alone. He'll have a whole graveyard to keep him company.

Once we're clear of any immediate threats, I spin myself around and look back at the remains of Fathomscape Station.

The outer ring is fully broken in half. The half we were on has twisted around to a ninety degree angle relative to its other half. The fires I used to be able to see through the windows on the middle ring have gone out, but it looks like the inner ring is now fully ablaze. Tiny views of the fire inside it twinkle redly in the distance, broken up and pixelated, as if each window were a single pixel in a piece of 8-bit art.

Ships hover at a distance, watching the wreckage. Many of them fly away. Most of them fly away. There are fewer and fewer ships in the area. I wonder if the new Ll'th'th queen is on one of those ships, setting off to start a new hive, somewhere else.

I wonder if the Ll'th'th queen is alive even. For all I know, her reign may have already come to an end. The Ll'th'th survivors may be picking yet another new queen right now. Each new queen enjoying a smaller court and looking forward to a shorter reign.

I hope some subset of their society survives, some central seed large enough to grow—elsewhere—into a new, healthy hive. I wish Kth had stayed alive to see it, to be a part of it. I didn't know her well, and I was uncomfortable with inviting her so completely into my home... but, well, geez. It's easier to think well of someone once they're dead, easier to look back and wish you'd done more, offered more, been more kind and giving.

I'll need to remember that when my family gets itself back together and I'm faced with the question of how to handle Kth's adopted daughter.

Kalithee is alone in this universe. Except for us. I just watched—and participated in—her actual genetic parent dying in the aftereffects of a grenade exploding, and before that... Well, I'm pretty damn sure Jaimy broke her adopted mother's neck.

Geez, in the story of Kalithee's life, we're the villains. We owe her. Even if her people destroyed my home, killed my beloved dog-daughter Gaby, infected and murdered my reptilian son A'nu and Jaimy's old companion Tyler... She didn't do any of that herself. She doesn't even know about any of it, except for—like the rest of us—missing A'nu.

She's ours. Whether we want her or not. Kalithee is ours. We're bound together by death and abandonment on both sides. It's an unholy marriage, but it still binds her to us, at least until we can find her a better home. And I'm not sure that for an abandoned foundling like her a better home than the one I can provide exists.

I guess, not unless we could actually take her home. To her homeworld. The world her people came from...

The place where the monsters began.

But that's a quest for another day.

Today, I need to find the rest of my family, huddling together in the void, and hope, hope, hope that our lifeboat boat returns for us.

16

The worst parts are over. I keep telling myself that as I float in the darkness, searching for my children and a child of my enemies, accompanied by Jaimy and two giant cubes in the darkness.

It takes a while to find Cristobel and the little ones. There aren't a lot of landmarks in the void around Fathomscape Station, just a lot of moving debris, flying every which way, creating a constantly changing, moving, unstable landscape. Basically, we're playing the worst game ever of Marco Polo.

But we have time.

We have as much time as our suits have air, and once we find her, if Cristy can figure out how to safely attach our suit tanks to the giant cubic tanks of compressed atmosphere, we have even more air than we have time. We have more air in those tanks than we can possibly use before dying from dehydration.

If *The Kanga* doesn't come back for us, eventually, we'll have to forage our way back through the wreckage, looking for supplies, looking for bubbles of safety, looking for anything that can be turned into a way to buy ourselves one more hour, one more day.

Because salvage ships will eventually come, and they will rescue the survivors.

What few survivors there will be.

I don't want us to be survivors though, merely waiting for rescue. I want us to be refugees who escaped this disaster aboard our own spaceship.

I want *The Kanga*. I want my home. I want my friend.

I want to lock myself in my own, private room and cry and cry and cry. I want to tell *The Kanga* all the fear I've been feeling, all the sadness that fills me like the glittering crystals inside a geode, sharp, angular, and bright. Almost beautiful, because the sadness is caused by memories of what was, what could have been if everything were different, and what I thought would be.

I was so very wrong.

I was afraid, but all my fears were wrong. Sure, some of the themes were right, but I could never have guessed this was how my life—hell, today, just today—that this was how today would play out.

I'm floating in a sea of sadness and the physical manifestation of my worst fears.

Over the suit radio, I listen to Max lead the others in singing Star-Shaker songs while we look for each other. He knows all the lyrics to every song by the s'rellick pop artist and says it'll be good for T'ni to learn songs by someone of his own species. Cristy sings along, but her voice doesn't have the purrful edge it usually does when she sings and she stumbles over the words. She doesn't know Star-Shaker's songs very well. Though, all of us have been learning. When you have a kid totally addicted to a particular pop artist, you can't help but learn.

Even Jaimy sings along in her gruff, booming voice. She sounds happier than I'd expect. Not happy, obviously. But like she's holding it together, which is amazing. I'm only passing for holding it together right now, because I'm not doing anything other than searching for my children, who I can hear are alive and vaguely safe. I'm not trying to sing.

Once we get ourselves all gathered together, I can see that Cristobel has tethered herself, Max, and the little ones all together. She's done a good job of keeping them safe, while Jaimy and I fetched a replacement atmosphere. Now we just need somewhere to put that atmosphere.

We need *The Kanga*.

I watch the yellow sun in the distance (dimmed by the reactive glass in my suit's helmet) and wait to see a shadow pass in front of it.

A *Kanga*-shaped shadow.

Neither T'ni nor Kalithee are really verbal yet, but my little reptile boy has been humming along with Max, who's still blithely singing. T'ni does seem to like Star-Shaker. Max is right about that.

As for Kalithee? She's been quiet this whole time. Like me. I don't know how much she understands. I don't know how attached she was or wasn't to Kth. Their relationship is a mystery to me, and even though Kalithee seems to have become mine—something I still hate and am still trying to find a way out of—I'll probably never know exactly what their relationship was. Kalithee is so young—even younger than T'ni—that I don't think she'll remember and be able to tell me, even when she can speak and explain.

Though I could be wrong about that. Her species maintains a shared, cultural memory passed down from parent to child. That's why I was able to learn so much about them when Ahn's-si's ghost passed through me. I was able to get a glimpse of what their world was like, what their society could have been, if they weren't starving and stranded.

Like T'ni, she's an unusual child. I guess, it makes sense for them to grow up together. Their oddities are connected. T'ni would never have hatched from an ancient egg—something so valuable that an entire team of s'rellick scientists came looking for him, braving the dangers of Hell Moon and losing their lives in the process—if his society hadn't disturbed the remains of Kalithee's society, stirring up monsters they couldn't survive.

Both children are relics of destroyed civilizations.

Looking out on the wreckage of Fathomscape Station, I realize: we all are now. Every one of us in my family is a survivor of a destroyed civilization.

Well, I hope we're survivors.

Max keeps brightly singing Star-Shaker's biggest hit—some insipid piece about shining her scales and not letting the haters drag her down. It's catchy. Max loves it. And right now, it's the only thing holding us together, keeping us from panicking as we wait.

I'm so grateful to Max for singing.

When he comes to a break between songs, I maneuver myself to where I can see his face through his helmet's face-plate and say, "Max, I didn't get a chance to tell you earlier—your haircut looks great."

My human child beams.

I'm keenly aware of how terrible the next few hours—and possibly the entire rest of our lives—could be if *The Kanga* never comes back, so the moment her voice crackles over my suit radio, I expect to burst into tears of relief. Instead, some-how, this seismic shift in possible futures—the difference between two entirely different paths; one filled with light and hope and the other filled with darkness, desperation, and pain —feels much smaller when it actually happens. Like I always knew she'd come back. Like all my doubts until that moment were silly. Overly dramatic. Because of course—*of course*—our ship has come home to us.

17

The *Kanga* flies straight to us. Her sensors are much better at zeroing in on our location than our suit sensors were for finding each other. Even so, I'm kind of impressed by how quickly she locates us, given all the noise that must be caused by the debris all around.

Her airlock is already open as she slides up beside us. She has no air inside her to protect right now. But also, it feels like she's eager to get us back aboard. Eager to have us home.

It must have been scary for her, having to leave us all behind like that. I don't say anything harsh about how she abandoned us. I don't remonstrate with her at all, say absolutely none of the cutting things I'd been planning. Instead, as I glide into the airlock with Jaimy and the children, I ask, "Did you get a nice tan?"

Cristobel stays outside with the tanks of compressed atmosphere. She offered to take charge of hooking them up and let Jaimy and me head back inside with the children first. Neither of us objected. Overall, I think she had an easier time of it, hanging out in the dark with Max leading campfire songs than, Jaimy and I had looting Fathomscape Station.

The two of us saw things during that mission we'll never unsee. As I stand in the airlock, still wearing a spacesuit, but finally, god finally, experiencing some reasonable gravity again, I catch Jaimy's eye. There's understanding there. We both know what we saw. We aren't going to want to talk about it.

"Actually," *The Kanga* says as our little group steps into her hallway and the double airlock doors shut behind us, "I believe I got more of a sunburn. After your unsettling news about mere vacuum not being strong enough to cure my infection, I wanted to be extra sure of coming away clean this time. So, I flew closer to the sun than was strictly safe."

A shiver runs up my spine as *The Kanga* says those words. I can't help picturing how differently everything would have gone—how different this exact moment would be—if she'd flown too close and fried some essential circuitry, leaving herself unable to fly away and instead slowly, slowly circling until she eventually fell into the sun.

She continues on to say, "I may need some minor repair work done, but nothing so essential it can't wait until we get to a safe, friendly star system."

I try to let out a sigh of relief. It comes out all shaky. I can't wait to take this spacesuit off and breathe some of the air Jaimy and I fought so hard for. I can't wait to give proper hugs to all my children.

"How long do you think it will take Cristobel to get the atmosphere tanks hooked up?"

"The first one is already hooked up," *The Kanga* answers. "I will have a breathable atmosphere available for you in about twenty minutes."

"Awesome," I reply, already counting the minutes until I'll be able to get something to eat. I'm starving. And exhausted. And worn-out. And scarred. And nothing will ever be the same again.

I lost another child today. I lost my childhood home.

But I'm here. Jaimy, Max, and the toddlers have already gone to the common area to play. I can still hear Max's voice ringing in my ears, playing over the suit radio.

I could follow them and watch, but instead, I take a minute for myself. I go to the bridge, because that's where I feel the most connected to *The Kanga*. I don't feel ready to talk to her yet. All those things I wanted to say—now that I could actually say them, I feel like bottling them up for later.

Instead, I sit down at the computer console Max was using earlier. In spite of my clumsily gloved hands, I manage to type in a few commands and call up informational files about the Ll'th'th.

I find a picture of one of their caterpillars. It *is* shaped a lot like Kalithee, at least in overall body structure. Long, squirmy body with two rows of too many stubby tentacle hands. Wriggling mouth parts. But instead of smooth, pale skin like Kalithee, the child in this picture is covered in weird globby spikes, and the whole thing is as bright orange as a gummy bear. Just like its parent and siblings, the caterpillar is colored like carnival candy.

I should have known better. I should have known Kalithee was adopted with a single glance.

And yet, should I? She could have been an unusual, unwanted, deformed child. One that the queen cast out, and so Kth took her in.

Even so, I can't believe I lived around Ll'th'th all my life, and I never thought to learn this simple thing about them. What their children look like.

It wouldn't have changed almost anything about today. I mean, I guess, maybe I'd have taken my whole family, cut and run, immediately upon seeing Kalithee if I'd known what she was, what her presence here in this star system meant.

And yet, I did know. Kind of. The moment I saw her, I thought of the maggots I'd seen in my vision. I thought of the murals I'd seen in those underground caverns. At some level, I knew, but I didn't trust myself. I couldn't trust myself, because I've been jumping at shadows for nine months, ever since Gaby died.

"Should I have known what Kalithee is?" I ask *The Kanga* over a private channel.

"Should *I* have known?" she asks in return. Before I can get too lost in pondering that, she adds, "You can take your suit off now."

So I do, and I go down to the common area where Jaimy, Max, and the toddlers have strewn their own spacesuits on the floor. We'll pick them up later. I sit down at the small table beside Jaimy and lean up against her. She puts an arm around me, and we just watch our children—two who we've known for nine months, and one we met today—play together in T'ni and A'nu's discarded egg shells.

Max brings us snacks, because he's that kind of thoughtful kid, still singing all the while. Eventually, Cristobel comes in from outside and joins us.

We're together. What's left of us. And that will have to be enough.

ABOUT THE AUTHOR

Mary E. Lowd is a prolific science-fiction and furry writer in Oregon. She's had more than 200 short stories and a dozen novels published, always with more on the way. Her work has won three Ursa Major Awards, ten Leo Literary Awards, and four Cóyotl Awards. She edited FurPlanet's ROAR anthology series for five years, and she is now the editor and founder of the furry e-zine *Zooscape*. She lives in a crashed spaceship, disguised as a house and hidden behind a rose garden, with an extensive menagerie of animals, some real and some imaginary.

For more information:
marylowd.com

To read Mary's short stories:
deepskyanchor.com

ALSO BY MARY E. LOWD

9 781088 298381